gossip
times
three

gossip times three

Amy Goldman Koss

DIAL BOOKS
New York

Published by Dial Books
A member of Penguin Group (USA) Inc.
345 Hudson Street
New York, New York 10014

Designed by Kimi Weart
Text set in Berkeley
Printed in the U.S.A. on acid-free paper

10 9 8 7 6 5 4 3

Library of Congress Cataloging-in-Publication Data

Koss, Amy Goldman, date.
Gossip times three / Amy Goldman Koss.
p. cm.
Summary: The relationships between three friends
change in seventh grade when they discover that two
of them have a crush on the same boy.
ISBN 0-8037-2849-2
[1. Friendship—Fiction.
2. Interpersonal relations—Fiction.]
I.Title.
PZ7.K8527 Go 2003
[Fic]—dc21
                                              2002010915

Many thanks to Lauri Hornik
for her smarts

and to Emily Koss,
Allison Kaliman,
and Sabrina Szymanski
for reasons I am not at liberty to discuss.

Prologue

IN THE NOBLE TRADITION of famous TRIOS (the THREE bears, THREE Musketeers, and THREE Stooges, as THREE examples), I bring you this true story about THREE best friends who will no doubt become my THREE sworn enemies when they find out that I'm writing this. Maybe I should say they're bunny rabbits, or rutabagas, so they won't recognize themselves. But vegetable parables are for cowardly writers, not brave gossips like myself.

We shall call the first of the THREE friends Abby because Abby starts with the first letter of the alphabet and that'll help you remember that she was the *first* girl to be in love with Zack. (Notice the Z.) So we've got A—Abby, and we'll name the other girls Bess (B) and Cristy (C), although I think Cristy is usually spelled with a K.

Chapter One

the beginning

THIS STORY BEGINS a few months into seventh grade, although Abby had been secretly carving Zack's name in her pajama drawer, and writing it in many other hidden (and not-so-hidden) places, since halfway through THIRD grade. If Abby had been offered THREE wishes, she wouldn't have had to give it a moment's thought. All THREE would've been for Zack to like her.

When anyone mentioned Romeo and Juliet, Abby automatically pictured herself and Zack. Valentines, smoochy TV programs, romantic perfume ads—all that made her think Zack! Zack! Zack! She even had a stuffed bear that she kissed good night, pretending it was him. And when she doodled (which was practically whenever there was a pencil and scrap of paper within reach), Abby wrote Zack's name and decorated it with hearts.

Not that Zack knew, or cared.

But Abby's best friends, Bess and Cristy (and this is important), *knew all about* Abby's long-standing crush. In fact, it was a big joke between them. Ha-ha, very funny.

Neither Bess nor Cristy had ever had a long crush. Bess had had multiple flash-crushes, lasting anywhere from THREE and a half seconds (on boys seen in line at the store) to nearly two weeks (on boys with actual names, at school). Bess's most recent "boyfriend" was Max, but we won't talk about that because it was *sooo* embarrassing!

Cristy, on the other hand, had not yet found herself gouging anyone's initials into her windowsill, or writing his last name over and over as her own. Not even a mini-crushette really. And to tell the truth, Cristy often wished her friends would go back to talking about something besides boys.

Then: Out of nowhere, before school on the second to last Tuesday of January, Bess said, "Zack's cute."

"Well, du-uh," Abby said, because she'd always thought Zack was cute (unbelievably cute, breathtakingly, mind-rattlingly cute), so she didn't immediately see why this was *news*. After her "Well, du-uh," she just went on with the (rather long) story she was telling.

But even though it didn't *look* like Bess's mention of Zack's cuteness made any impression on Abby, it must have, because at lunch, THREE hours later, when Bess said, "Zack has a goofy smile," Abby started getting a stomachache. The deep, low kind. The "oh no" kind. The kind of stomachache that makes you hunch over and moan. The kind that no heating pad or chalky medicine will help.

But Abby didn't hunch over or moan or go to the school nurse in search of chalky medicine.

Wait. Let's back up to Bess's *first* mention of Zack's cuteness (before the lunchtime, bellyache-inducing comment on his goofy smile), and here's why we're backing up: It occurs to me that Bess's Zack comment probably wasn't the very beginning of the story, because before Bess could *say* Zack was cute, she had to have thought it.

I suppose it's *possible* (although not very likely) that Bess suddenly noticed that Zack was cute just split seconds before she mentioned it (the way we don't have to spend a lot of time formulating the expression "Ouch!" when we burn ourselves).

But maybe she'd been making mental note of Zack and his cuteness for hours, or even days! For all I know I might have been totally wrong on page four when I said Bess had never had a long crush. Maybe she'd had a secret crush on Zack for as long as Abby had. Think of the self-control it would've taken for Bess to bite her tongue (ouch!) and suffer silently all that time! It must've been murder to listen (or even *half*-listen) to Abby download endlessly about Zack.

As a matter of fact, that's *precisely* what Abby was doing at the very second Bess interrupted her to say, "Zack's cute."

Here's how it went. Abby: "So, he's handing out the math quizzes, right? And I was counting the seats till he'd reach me? And I'm sooo glad I wore my blue shirt, because imagine if I'd worn that yellow one! Gross! I'd totally die. You know, that stupid yellow striped *thing*? My mom has been snails with the laundry lately and I've *no* idea what's up with *that,* but out of total desperation I swear I had the yellow shirt *in my hand*! And I came *this* close to putting it on because I was all, who cares what I wear? I practically never see Zack anyway, half the time."

Cristy wasn't even pretending to listen. She was balancing her binder on her head with only minor success. And there was poor, long-suffering Bess, nodding (when appropriate) as Abby went on (and on and on).

"But my guardian angel must've been on duty or whatever, 'cause I found the blue one all mashed at the bottom of my drawer. Not that it's *gorgeous,* exactly, but think of the yellow one!" Abby shuddered. "So, anyway, he's walking down the rows and he gets to my seat, right? And he like gives me the test? And he almost practically *smiles* right at me, and I totally *die*! Can you imagine?"

Bess nodded. Secretly, she would've given anything on earth just to sniff a math quiz that had been touched by Zack, her secret love! But not a soul (except maybe Bess's big sister, Gilda, but probably not even her) knew a thing about Bess's secret romantic agony.

Then, unable to bear it any longer, Pow! Out of Bess's mouth exploded the fateful words "Zack's cute." Oh no! There it was! Blurted for all the world to hear!!!

But Cristy didn't hear it because she automatically tuned out her friends when they got to flapping their lips about boys. And Abby was so caught up in the story she was telling, about Zack handing back the quizzes, that all she said in reaction to Bess's explosion was, "Well, du-uh," and she kept going with her monologue.

As I said before, anything's possible. But I really *don't* think that's how it went. For one thing, I've known Bess all her life and can say with absolute certainty that she's not the kind of girl to keep *anything* (let alone a giant crush) to herself. Bess is the type who's *got* to announce "You should see how much gunk was in the zit I just popped!" or "I've got a wedgie" in situations where no one else would feel the need to share that information.

And for another thing, just last Thursday Bess was crazy about a boy named Max, although that's an entirely different story. (Remind me to tell you about it later.)

Chapter One
and a THIRD

details

BUT POOR STOMACHACHING ABBY. It had never even *occurred* to her to worry about anyone else noticing Zack's cuteness or his goofy smile. And if she *had* worried about someone noticing him, she never, ever, ever would've suspected that the someone could be Bess!

This whole stinky situation sounds like the kind of thing a girl would run home to talk over with her mom in a sunny kitchen that smells of cinnamon rolls baking. A kitchen with daisies, not crusty breakfast dishes, on the table. And no overflowing trash cans in the background either.

The troubled daughter (Abby) would confide to her sympathetic mother: "Me and my best friend like the same boy!"

"Oh dear," the mother would wisely soothe. "That *is* a pickle!"

Note: The mother would *not* say, "You call that a problem, when people are dying of oozing diseases all over the globe?" Nor would Mom say, "Awww, that's so pwecious! You have a wittle boyfwend!"

Be that as it may, it's entirely possible that Abby *would have* discussed the whole Bess-Zack-Abby TRIANGLE with her mom if she'd had a chance. But she didn't, and I'll tell you why in a minute, but first I should explain something: Abby's parents are divorced.

Yes, it's true that divorce neither makes it impossible to bake cinnamon rolls nor causes trash to overflow. But for the next part of this story to make sense, you have to know that Abby's mom is single. And now is as good a time as any to tell you that Bess's and Cristy's parents are divorced too. It's an amazing coincidence, but there it is.

For a while the THREE girls considered calling themselves the D of D (Daughters of Divorce). Or the DDD, (*Dashing* Daughters of Divorce, or Daring or Divine or Darling—anything but Dull). But Bess Decided it sounded Desperately Depressing and Cristy thought it was Dorky.

The thing is: You know that legend where two women were fighting over a baby and asked Abraham or Solomon or some wise Bible dude to settle it, and his advice was to cut the kid in half? Well, Abby's parents must've been called to the phone at that point in the story, because they obviously missed the part where the cutting in half was majorly *not okay* with the *real* mom—the point being that moms, as a general rule, *don't* go in for hacking up their kids.

In other words, Abby's mom (and dad) thought the half-and-half idea sounded just peachy. They didn't chop Abby's actual *body* in half, but they hacked her life to bits, and her little brother Spencer's, and their pug dog Wheezy's too. Because the best plan they could come up with was to *share* by forcing their kids and dog to careen forth and back from one parent's house to the other. Wake up Monday morning at Mom's. Go to sleep that night at Dad's. One weekend Mom's house through lunch on Saturday, Dad's till Sunday dinner. Then the next weekend, switch, unless it's a holiday . . . No wonder Wheezy often forgot where exactly she *was*—and was *not*—supposed to pee.

But even though Abby was at her mom's place the night of the day that Bess said she thought Zack was cute and had a goofy smile, Abby did *not* tell her mom about it because: 1) (as I told you before) Abby didn't get a chance, and 2) Abby's mom was acting weird.

What was she doing? Changing her clothes.

It was like this: When she came home from work, instead of heading for the fridge like she usually does, Abby's mom ran around scooping up toys, towels, dishes, and clothes while yelling commands like, "Abby! Wipe the kitchen table and brush your hair. Spency! Make sure both toilets are flushed . . ."

Then she dove in and out of the shower and started yanking clothes from her closet. Abby watched her mom dress, undress, and dress again. Mom's explanation was that "a friend from work is bringing carryout for dinner."

"What kind of carryout?" Spencer asked, as if *that* were the important part.

"What kind of *friend*?" Abby asked (more to the point).

"Just a friend-friend. His name's Steve," her mom answered, whipping off another sweater and digging through a drawer. But Abby knew that no one changes her sweater fifty times for a friend-friend.

Then Abby's mom set the table with the *breakable* dishes.

If we were talking about *Bess's* mom, it would be a different story. Bess's mom (whose name is Lindy and who everyone including Bess calls by her first name) dated like crazy and was either sickeningly in love or heartsick with disappointment at all times. And in spite of the fact that the expression "unlucky in love" was invented for people like her, Lindy never gave up.

But we weren't talking about *Bess's* mom. We were talking about *Abby's* mom, whose divorce (THREE years ago) had stung so so so badly that she hadn't been on a single solitary date since. Not even a half date, or an on-line cyber-flirtation. So you can see why Abby's mom's daughter Abby was too freaked by the prospect of friend-friend Steve coming over to mention the Zack-Bess thing. Not that her mom was in any state of mind to listen, busy as she was changing sweaters. And they didn't have daisies on their table anyway, so forget it.

Interruption: Ding-dong! (Abby's doorbell.) "Bark! Bark!" (Wheezy.) Enter Steve.

He was tall. Very tall. He practically had to dip his head to get through the kitchen door. He made the bags of Chinese food look tiny. Spencer and Abby were speechless. No living thing that size had ever come through their door before.

Spencer asked, "Are you a giant?" (He's six and can get away with saying stuff like that.)

Steve didn't seem to mind. He answered, "Not technically."

Then Spencer asked Steve if he got his shoes in a regular shoe store, and Abby looked down and saw the biggest feet of her life. Abby's mom shot Spencer a "That's enough!" look. But Steve told them that he had to order his shoes special, through the mail.

"I bet no one ever picked fights with you," Spencer said.

"To tell you the truth," Steve said, "it was quite the opposite. Kids always wanted to beat me up to prove they could whoop the big guy. If it hadn't been for my big brothers, I would've spent my entire childhood fighting."

Spencer's jaw dropped. "Your *big* brothers?" he asked, and even Abby's mom cracked up.

Steve had brought all their favorite dishes, so Abby figured he must've asked Mom what she and Spencer liked.

But the whole dinner, with Steve sitting so hugely on their little kitchen chair, was so weird that Abby for once didn't totally pig on the sweet and sour. She just ever-so-carefully isolated each bit of bell pepper (which she detested and despised more than any other food on earth), and after banishing every speck to her wadded-up napkin, she picked at the rest with her chopsticks, as delicately as a princess.

Perhaps you're wondering why I told you so many details about this one evening: the dishes, Steve's shoe size, etc. Especially since I didn't do that for any other scene. For instance, have I told you whether or not there were flowers on Bess's or Cristy's kitchen table? No, I haven't told you (but no, there were not).

Last Valentine's Day there were, though, when Bess's big sister, Gilda, got a dozen pink roses from a boy in her biology lab. Unfortunately Gilda thought he was a jerk. It's such a shame when some romantic thing happens for the first time with the wrong guy. Not to mention what a drag it must be to *be* the wrong guy trying to do a romantic thing, not knowing that your romantic thing is totally unwanted. But the trickiness of boy-girl mis-understandings is not the point. And the roses were nice, although for future reference, Gilda would've preferred yellow or even red. Actually, anything *but* pink (which totally proves how little the guy in her biology lab understood her).

But I got descriptive about the Steve-coming-to-Abby's-house scene for other reasons—THREE actually. Number one is that a realistic bit of dialogue and home life will prove to you that I *totally* know these girls inside out and am not making this up. And 2) the green pepper business is *foreshadowing* something I'm going to tell you later, if I don't forget. And the THIRD reason is, well, never mind that one because the *most* important part is this: The next day (at school) Abby said, "My mom had a guy over last night," making Bess's and Cristy's eyeballs pop right out of their heads.

Cristy found her voice first and said, "Your mom? A *guy?*"

"A *date* kind of guy?" Bess asked, amazed.

Abby shrugged. "I guess so. He brought dinner."

"Did your mom loon out? Act all giggly? Extra chipper?" Bess asked. "That's how you can tell if he was a *guy* or just a guy."

"She didn't act that weird," Abby said. "But she used the good dishes."

Bess and Cristy considered that.

"And she changed her clothes about twelve times before he got there," Abby added.

"That's a date!" Bess shrieked. "I'm in shock!"

Then Cristy asked, "Was he nice?"

Abby nodded. "Yeah."

"You're new at this," Bess scoffed. "Take it from a pro— he was faking. Trying to impress you so you'll tell your mom you think he's great. They always do that in the beginning."

Which reminded all THREE girls of horrible, hated (boo-hiss) Jonas. He doesn't have tons to do with this story, so I'll just quickly tell you that a while back, Bess and her big sister, Gilda, and most of all their mom, Lindy, thought a guy named (boo-hiss) Jonas (before the boo-hiss was added to his name) was going to be Capital *I*, Capital *T*—IT. Lindy had even snuck *Bride* magazines into the apartment.

They all thought (b-h) J was the sweetest, coolest, funniest, most terrificest man on the planet—and he turned out to be, well, *not.*

It was majorly nauseating for Bess and her big sister, Gilda, to remember how they raced each other to the door whenever Jonas came over. And (gag!) they used to throw their arms around his neck! Maybe that memory turned Bess's stomach a little less than it did Gilda's, since Bess wasn't as sensitive to humiliation as Gilda was—as proven by Bess's whole Max thing, which I swore I'd never tell anyone about so don't ask.

Remembering (boo-hiss) Jonas brought up the subject of Bess's mom's love life. And even though it doesn't have much to do with this situation either (meaning the situation regarding Bess thinking Abby's lifelong crush Zack was cute), I might as well tell you what the girls said after they said the stuff about Abby's mom having a guy over last night and it being a date.

But first you should know that the conversation about Steve, which reminded everyone of (b-h) J, took place in the school "lunchroom," which is not really a room since it doesn't have walls, and walls are considered by many people to be a fairly essential component of something if it's going to be called a *room*. In fact, I bet the word *wall* is part of the definition of the word *room*. Something like: A room is a structure with walls and a roof and usually a door.

The "lunchroom" *does* have a roof, which would probably almost keep the kids dry if there were fewer of them crammed under it. But luckily, it rarely rains during the school year here. And the reason I've told you all *that* is because sometimes it's good to know where the girls are so you can picture them. It's called *setting the scene*. And it answers the *where?* in the *who? what? where? when? why?* that we narrators are supposed to concern ourselves with constantly, according to my writing teacher, Mr. Wordsmith.

Anyway, here's what was going on: Cristy had arranged all her little containers (tortellini, lemon yogurt, sliced kiwi, and oyster crackers, to be exact) in a half circle around her. Next she reached over and nabbed half of Abby's baloney sandwich, saying "sand-switch" at the same time as Abby called "turtle-beanies" and plucked the tortellini container out of Cristy's careful half circle.

This was tradition. And Bess, also according to tradition, was eating her own lunch, sharing not one chip. By the way, don't you think it's odd that Cristy gets up extra early every morning to carefully pack an interesting lunch—that she doesn't eat?

Okay, now we've set the scene and we're ready—unless you need to know what they were wearing, in which case I'll tell you quickly (but honestly) that all THREE of them wore identical jeans that they'd bought on sale at the exact same time, like TRIPLETS. But I have to draw the line there, because if we start discussing their shoes and shirts and hair thingies, I'm afraid we'll get so sidetracked that their lunch hour will end and we'll have missed the rest of the conversation. Especially since their lunch hour is really only forty-five minutes.

So, forget their clothes, and no makeup was allowed at their school, so don't even ask me about the suspicious redness of Abby's lips or the strange shimmeriness on all six of their eyelids.

For all we know the pink on Bess's cheeks could've been a fever developing, or perhaps she was thinking about the cuteness of Zack. On the other hand, Bess may have been flushed by the subject she was about to raise. It's entirely possible, you know, that her mom's dating situation was more upsetting than she let on.

In any case the conversation began, or rather continued, with Bess saying, "Lindy is in love."

"Again?" Abby asked.

"With who?" asked Cristy, her mouth full of lunch.

Bess shrugged. "His name's Eric. I haven't met him yet. Lindy says she's not going to introduce me to him because she's sure I'll like him so much that if they ever broke up I'd go mad with grief and run in circles shrieking and tearing my hair out. Which they won't, of course, according to her."

"Won't what? Break up?" Abby asked.

"Right. Because this Eric guy is so great." Bess rolled her eyes and gave a little snort.

Cristy piped up with, "Lindy's right, though. All the magazine articles on 'How to Be a Good Divorced Mom and Not Screw Your Kids Up Any More than Absolutely Necessary' say they're supposed to keep their boyfriends away from us until they're sure he's Prince Charming."

Bess sighed. "Yeah, but my mom's positive that every guy she meets is happily-ever-after, walk-down-the-aisle, till-death-do-us-part material."

Cristy and Abby nodded. They'd known Lindy (Bess's mom) forever as the wholehearted, headfirst, this-time-is-completely-different type.

Bess went on. "Lindy's now listening to the tortured-bug music this Eric person likes. And she's eating his lumpy health clay for breakfast. Blacch! And you know the painting of cows in the living room?"

Cristy and Abby nodded some more.

"Well, Eric hated it, so Lindy took it down. The cows are hiding behind the couch now, facing the wall."

"I liked the cows," Abby said, wondering if Steve was going to make her mom redecorate.

"Me too," Cristy said, eyeing Abby's last cookie.

"Eric thinks they're too cute," Bess said.

"What's wrong with cute?" asked Abby.

Cristy nabbed the cookie, saying, "Your mom's cute and he likes her."

"My mom is not cute," Bess said, getting huffy.

"She is too," Cristy insisted.

"Will someone please tell me what's wrong with cute?" repeated Abby.

But no one did. Each of them mulled over the anti-cuteness puzzle in her own way, and chewed. After a while Bess said, "Oh, and Lindy changed her hair color again yesterday. Now she's a redhead. Well, sort of an orange-head, actually."

Cristy rolled her eyes, but Abby automatically wondered if Zack would pay attention to her if she dyed her hair orange. Almost every mention of anything made Abby wonder something or other about Zack. But if I typed them all into this story, it would get way too tedious and repetitive, so from now on just assume that Abby is thinking about Zack like background music or like how you don't even notice that you're constantly hearing something (the hum of a neighbor's air conditioner or freeway traffic).

But besides wondering about the possible effect on Zack of orange hair, Abby also secretly bet Lindy looked really cute as an orange-head. Then she caught herself and wondered if cuteness-wise, orange hair was dangerous.

Are you keeping the THREE mothers straight here? Let's review, because although the plot of this story is about the THREE girls, the subplot is about their moms.

And in case you wondered why none of the moms have names of their own (besides Lindy), it's because I think you already have enough names to keep straight and in a few pages you'll have even more. So you should thank me.

Oh, okay, for those of you who can't stand missing pieces, Abby's mom is named Sandy Falzetta, and Cristy's mom's name is Ms. Levine. (I swear I'd tell you her first name if I knew it.) Now let's just go back to calling them Abby's mom and Cristy's mom, all right?

1) Abby's mom was the one who had tall Steve over last night. It was Abby whose parents had the Ping-Pong custody of her and her dog and her brother. Luckily (and I forgot to tell you this earlier), her parents' houses were only THREE and a half blocks apart.

2) Bess's parents have been divorced forever. Bess's mom (Lindy, the orange-head, who was now giddy over a New-Agey guy named Eric) was the most glamorous of the THREE moms. She was always fashionably dressed and polished and painted. Bess also had a big sister, Gilda, who we know almost nothing about, which is a tragic oversight that should be taken care of immediately!

Gilda . . . where to begin? She's so complex. Funny but serious. Down to earth but not dumpy. Kind but not a chump. She's sixteen. Her favorite color is purple, and her favorite book is *The Little Prince*. She knows it by heart. She refuses to take anyone seriously who hasn't read it, and she wouldn't even consider being friends with any-

one who didn't love it, so before you go any further you might want to jot down this title: *The Little Prince* by Antoine De Saint-Exupéry, which is a hard name to pronounce unless you're French.

But in the meantime, I think we'd better get back to our discussion of parental situations. Starting with, or continuing with, Lindy's ex-husband (Bess and Gilda's dad), who moved to another city in another state (Farmington Hills, Michigan, to be exact, which is a suburb of Detroit) ages and ages ago. Bess and Gilda go there over school vacations, but once in a blue moon he shows up in town. At least he used to. Come to think of it, the last time was Bess's birthday party almost THREE years ago, and that didn't go so great.

The impression is that Bess's dad dates a ton in Michigan. Mostly younger women—like way younger. Like practically just a few years older than his oldest daughter, Gilda. Well, not really, but you know what I mean.

In any case, as of this writing, Bess and Gilda's dad has not read *The Little Prince,* in spite of having been given a copy for Father's Day last year. I think that says something about him, don't you?

3) (THREE) Cristy's mom—we haven't gotten to her yet, but in brief, she went out with a man a few years ago, but that relationship seemed to have bored itself to death. No tears, no fight, just sort of blah. She hasn't been out with anyone since then, unless it was in secret while Cristy was in school. Or maybe Cristy's mom snuck out

at night when Cristy was sleeping! But I really, really, *really* don't think so, and here's why:

It has been my observation that a certain amount of frantic fuss and shrieking always precedes dates. Running from room to room looking for shoes, yelling at people for not returning hairbrushes, etc. And Cristy's mom always looks so settled in and comfy that there's no way she's about to jump up and dash off anywhere.

If she isn't curled up with a cat, reading on the living room hammock, or reading at the table, oblivious to everything around her, absentmindedly letting the soup dribble off the spoon halfway to her mouth, then she's soaking up to her chin in the tub, getting the pages of some book soggy. (There are always swollen paperbacks drying on windowsills.)

For as long as anyone can remember, Cristy's dad has been (re)married to a nice woman with THREE older kids from a previous marriage who Cristy doesn't hate or resent. In fact, when she had to write an essay in sixth grade on someone she admired, she wrote about her fun-loving stepsister! And her fun-loving stepsister was so flattered and pleased that she had the essay framed. Can you imagine?

And Cristy and her mom and her dad and her stepmother and everyone all get together for happy holidays. The whole thing could be a how-to handbook on perfectly blended families. The title would be: *Sensible, Well-Adjusted People Being Good to Each Other,* with the subtitle *A Totally Inspiring Real-Life Example for Us All.*

Note: Besides happy holidays, Cristy sees her dad for dinner on Wednesdays, and every other weekend, except during football season.

(If you are still not totally clear on who's who in the mom department, I'll wait here while you go back and read that part over.)

Chapter One and a Half

zipped lips

*N*OW LET'S SKIP *AHEAD* THREE days (from when the girls were in the "lunchroom" discussing Abby's mom's "date" with Steve, and Bess's mom's orange hair and new boyfriend Eric) to when Bess marched right up to Zack in front of his locker and said (out loud and in English), "I like you." Just like that.

And (as Bess reported back to her dumbstruck pals moments later) Zack replied, "I like you too." And they became boyfriend and girlfriend.

I can't personally picture this conversation taking place *exactly* like that, with no um's or well's or whatever's, but that's the way it was reported.

Anyway, unless you're unconscious, you can probably imagine how Abby felt when she heard about this . . . this

confession of *like,* this romantic chat, this sneaky betrayal, or whatever you want to call it. Well, I don't know precisely, for sure, how she felt, but I'm willing to bet that her brain became one big, echoing *Huh? What? Huh???*

(Note: Jealousy is a very tricky emotion that brings out the best in no one on earth—but that doesn't stop us or anybody else from feeling it. The question becomes, Do we keep our unattractive [in fact, *ugly*] little feelings to ourselves, or share them? Abby chose *not* to share.)

She (Abby) was stunned, stupefied, flabbergasted, and blown away that one of her very best friends was now her crush's *girlfriend.* Who even knew that Zack was *interested* in having a girlfriend in the first place?

In addition to being stunned, etc., Abby felt majorly *ticked off* (and who wouldn't?) that best-friend Bess went after Zack knowing full well that Abby was totally in love with him and always had been. And whether or not Zack liked Abby *back* had nothing at all to do with it. Abby considered him hers, meaning off-limits, if not to the whole world of girls, at least to her *best girlfriends*!

Eew. The entire situation totally reeked, and Abby wanted to crawl into a hole and hide. She didn't have an actual hole to crawl into, though. No cave. No ditch. Not even an available closet. The only thing she could do was disappear inside her own skin by keeping her face *blank* and her mouth shut.

I would have . . . Well, I'm not sure what I would've done if I'd been Abby. I like to think I would've told Bess off at least, in some clever, quotable way. Or maybe I would have . . . who knows? But I would've done *something*. Wouldn't you? Even if it was something as lame and weenie as bursting into tears?

But even if you'd been watching Abby's face *very* closely for coloring or expression changes, you wouldn't have picked up the least clue that she gave a single, solitary Fig Newton about the whole "I like you—I like you too" business. So to be fair, how was Bess supposed to know how Abby felt???

Maybe if Abby had *said something* (like, How dare you? or even, Hey! I liked him first!) when Bess said Zack was cute, or when she (Abby) got that very first stomachache over Bess saying Zack had a goofy smile, then this whole skanky boyfriend-girlfriend thing wouldn't have happened. But having chosen silence *then,* and rechoosing silence *now*—what could Abby expect?

There is a lesson here: You have to *tell* people how you feel if you want them to know.

Plus, in the long run, it would've been better for *Bess* if Abby had said something like "Back off!" or "You're way out of line here!" to help Bess learn the rules. But, of course, people break these rules left and right, and that's how come you hear about dads running off with baby-sitters and moms being caught smooching with video clerks and tennis coaches. But still, as civilized people we're supposed to at least *try* not to go after other people's boyfriends or husbands or whatever, right?

Anyway, by now you're probably wondering where *Cristy* was in all this. Well, if you thought it was easier to be Cristy, you're right. But eas*ier* in this case doesn't necessarily mean *easy*. Because whether or not Abby was flipping out (on the inside) about the Bess/Zack development, Cristy was having her own TRIATHLON of panic.

Her first panic was, Uh-oh! What's it going to do to our TRIO if they both like the same guy? Break us all apart?

Then along came her second panic: Boyfriend-girlfriend? Again? Hasn't Bess had enough of that? Is this the way it's going to be from now on? Ick. The whole thing seems so retarded.

Now, don't be mad at Cristy for not considering *Abby's* pain right now. It's not that she doesn't care. It's just that Bess and Abby (pain or not) are on the same side of this particular fence, bringing us neatly to panic number THREE, where Cristy thinks, Is it *me*? Am *I* missing something here??? It sure seems like everybody else is in on it. Everyone gets the joke, knows the secret handshake and the secret password but me! Feels like they're all winking and nudging each other and trying not to laugh in front of poor dumb clueless *me*. A thousand icks!

When had everyone else stopped dog-paddling and learned the breaststroke? Cristy wondered breathlessly. And speaking of *breasts,* Cristy couldn't help noticing that both Bess and Abby had more to talk about on *that* subject too.

Chapter One and Two THIRDs

ritual celebration

*F*OR BESS, the fun of having a fresh new boyfriend started immediately. Within seconds of the spoken "I like you—I like you too" exchange, Bess got to bask in the priceless expressions on Abby's and Cristy's faces. And then she could see the news spreading like waves through the boys in the hallway. Zack's best buds started thumping him on the head, then ramming into him in a sort of primitive celebration that escalated into chicken fights, with some boys on other boys' shoulders and all of them trying to knock everyone else over to splat in bloody mayhem on the hard floor. (This male ritual was stopped by the PE teacher's shrill whistle followed by his offer to herd them all into the principal's office.)

The girls were much less rowdy about the news.

Mostly they just marveled and whispered and tossed their hair around, each girl privately considering the love floating freely through the air, which could settle like fairy dust on one of them next.

Bess felt eyes, hundreds of boy eyes and girl eyes, checking her out, thinking of her as Zack's girlfriend. And thank goodness! Now everyone would forget that whole horribly humiliating mess between her and her last "boyfriend," Max. (I swear I'd tell you about that, but we don't have time right now and anyway, Bess would kill me.)

So then, the icing on the cake, meaning the perfect end to the perfect day, was this: Right before the school-end bell when Zack flung a crumpled note to Bess, Ms. MacDooley intercepted it, and read it to the class—her grown-uppedness and authority making it the public announcement that turned Zack and Bess into an official Couple with a Capital *C*.

Meeting at Abby's locker after school, Bess said, "I could've died! I mean, I've never been so embarrassed in my entire life! Can you *believe* Ms. Mac read it out loud?"

Cristy shook her head in loyal disbelief and grunted sympathetically.

Abby busily made double sure her homework sheet was in her binder.

"Can you imagine how Zack felt?" Bess asked, scanning over her friends' heads to see who else was around, and wondering if Zack was going to be the kind of boyfriend who came over after school or what.

"He must have died!" Cristy answered, hoping that was the right line, for the right cue. She looked at Abby, but there were no hints there. Abby seemed to be lost in her own thoughts, scraping a crusty stain off her sleeve with a fingernail. Then Abby fixed her shoe.

"So," Cristy finally thought to ask, "what did Zack's note say?" (Cristy had been at chorus when it happened.)

"Oh, nothing really," Bess said, blushing.

That blush proved that Cristy was doing it right and gave her the inspiration to bump Bess's shoulder and say, "Come on, tell!"

Bess protested awhile, then said, "Oh, you know, something about, like, 'Hi,' and stuff like that. Really nothing." And she grinned from head to toe.

Chapter One
and Two THIRDs
(continued)

shivers

THIS WAS A CREEPY MOMENT: Abby, Cristy, and Bess were cruising the mall later that day, when a blue shirt caught Abby's eye and she automatically thought, *Zack would like that,* at precisely the same split second that Bess spoke the exact same, identical words ("Zack would like that") out loud.

Abby clamped her hand over her mouth and writhed in red-hot agony, wondering if she'd *said* that or *thought* it. Don't you hate when that happens? It's no mystery, as far as the shirt itself goes, that both girls thought of Zack when they saw it, because he always wore blue shirts just like the one in the shop window. But that's not the point. The point is, Abby knew that she was not supposed to have studied her best friend's boyfriend closely enough to know what he wore. Even if Abby herself had loved him with all her heart since THIRD grade, and even if he'd only been Bess's boyfriend since lunchtime.

Abby vowed up and down (on the inside) to be way more careful—to get Zack out of her head, even if it took brainwashing. Not that she knew how to wash her brain, though she suspected it had something to do with loud, repetitive noises like the chopping of wood. Maybe she should fill her cranium with cranked-to-the-hilt head-banging tunes on headphones, she thought. Or maybe brains were washed by the kind of chanting that Bess's mom, Lindy, was going to start doing (at new boyfriend Eric's suggestion) sometime in chapter five. In any case, Zack's shirts were no longer Abby's business (not that they really ever were), and Abby was quite firm with herself on that topic.

That very night, back home after the mall and dinner and after Spencer had gone to bed, Abby and her mom had this conversation:

Abby: "How'd you get rid of Dad?"

Mom: "I beg your pardon?"

Abby: "I mean from your head."

Mom: (yawning) "What are you asking me here, Ab?"

Abby: (getting exasperated) "Just what I said. How did you get Dad out of your thoughts?"

Mom: "Is this one of those important mother-daughter talks? Because if it's *not*, I'd really like to get in the shower."

Abby: "Mom!"

Mom: "What?"

Abby: "Never mind, okay? Just *forget it!* And forgive me for breathing, for Pete's sake!"

No, wait. *That's* not the conversation I meant. The one I had in mind was much, much cozier. But for all its warm, sympathetic fuzziness, that one wasn't any help *either.* Because in spite of Abby's mom's best intentions, all she could come up with advice-wise was "Time heals all."

Chapter One and THREE Quarters

looks

I JUST REALIZED that I haven't told you what these girls look like. Appearance is totally unimportant, of course, compared to personality, inner beauty, and moral character. But in case you're curious, or so you can recognize them if you run into them at the mall, I'll try to describe them.

This bit doesn't move the plot forward, though, so you can skip it if you want.

1) Abby is really cute.

2) Bess is pretty cute too, but in a different way.

Some people think 3) (THREE) Cristy is the cutest of the THREE, but other people don't think so at all.

Hair: I personally think Bess has the best hair—thick, shiny, black (like her sister Gilda's), going back to a Vietnamese grandmother on their dad's side. But there's nothing at all wrong with Cristy's wavy blond hair, although it bugs me to death when she chews on it. And seeing the wet strands hanging down her back after being chewed grosses me totally out.

And Abby's (brown) hair would look pretty, or at least it wouldn't look so stringy, if she'd just brush it once in a while and get her bangs out of her eyes. Which she does later in this story in a fairly drastic way, as you will see in chapter nine.

Bess and Cristy both have really pretty eyes (brown). Not that Abby's aren't pretty too. They totally are.

Cristy has an adorable turned-up nose. It's only fair, though, to remind you that noses like that (no offense) can sometimes, from a certain angle, look kind of piggy later on some adults.

Bess is the only one with incredibly long eyelashes.

Abby has braces.

Bess looks a tiny bit less cute when she slouches and does her bored, foot dragging thing.

Cristy thinks she's fat, but she's not. And that's it.

Chapter Two

denial

WE ARE NOW at Abby's dad's house at bedtime the next night. He thinks she's sound asleep, but you probably think she's obsessing about Zack and Bess and weeping into Wheezy's fur. Well, you're both wrong. Abby's listening to The Blue Bruise on headphones and sewing orange beads onto her lamp shade in the pattern of a smiling sun.

Earlier in the evening she'd solemnly removed page after page from books, notebooks, diaries, address books, calendars, etc., that had Zack's name doodled on them. Then, slipping into her dad's office she'd fed the whole shebang to his paper shredder. She didn't cry or even sigh all that much while doing it, nor did she say any final kind of crush-ending or funeralish things. She just shredded.

And except for sneaking an occasional guilty peek over

her shoulder (because she's not exactly *allowed* to use her dad's shredder without permission and supervision), she actually felt more or less okay.

That is because Abby is now in denial, and I can't resist saying, "De Nile ain't just a river in Egypt!" Actually, eight other countries besides Egypt rely on the Nile for water. We here in North America take our fresh water for granted, especially those of us who live in places like Wisconsin and Minnesota, where there's practically a lake on every corner.

But lakes and rivers and melting snowcaps are not evenly distributed around the globe, and many dry, dusty countries have to have wars and kill each other's citizens over measly puddles. What that has to do with my story is this: Taking things for granted is a dangerous luxury. In this case the taking of granteds are these:

1) Abby had *mistakenly* taken it for granted that her friends understood that she had eternal dibs on Zack.

2) Cristy took it for granted that if there was a problem, someone would speak up and say so. Therefore, since no one talked about a problem, there *was* no problem!

3) (THREE) Bess took it for granted that no matter what insensitive, selfish, and downright mean things she did (yes, even if she went after Abby's crush like a shark after a wounded surfer, without so much as asking permission or offering an apology), they'd all stay best friends forever and ever.

And for now, thanks to Abby's *denial,* it looked, smelled,

tasted, and sounded like Bess was right. She *was* going to get away with it. And if we peeked in on her (Bess) right now, we'd see an angelic sleeping girl, curled up with her beloved (though tattered) stuffed rabbit, Bun-Bun, dreaming the happy, guiltless dreams of the innocent. So there you are.

Note regarding Abby's denial: When Abby told her dad that she was going along with Bess to Zack's soccer game, because Zack wanted *Bess* to watch him play, Abby's dad said, "Is that the same Zack whose name you wrote in pimple cream on the mirror?"

And (here's the denial part) Abby rolled her eyes and said, "No, *Daaaaad*. Sheesh!"

P.S. She didn't tell him about her mom's new "friend" Steve either.

Any questions?

Chapter THREE

a terribly important chapter

THIS IS THE THIRD CHAPTER of this tale of THREE friends. And by the time this story is finished, there will have been at least THREE major plot twists in THIRTEEN chapters. Isn't that chillingly THREEish?

Lots of people think the strongest things come in THREES. Carpenters use TRIANGLES of wood as supports in building. Cameras and telescopes are supported on TRIPODS. We use TRIPLE digits to call for help: 911 and SOS.

But in spite of all those hearty THREES, ***THREE-SOMES in friendship can be very wobbly!*** (Note: I **bold-faced,** *italicized,* and underlined that because it's terribly important for you to understand how terribly important that fact is.) So don't say I didn't warn you.

Nonetheless, as of the beginning of chapter THREE, the THREE friends (Abby, Bess, and Cristy) still looked solid. Here's a paragraph (or THREE) on each of them:

Cristy was getting used to the new world with boyfriends in it. As long as it only meant having to sit around while Bess made the occasional phone call to Zack, it was bearable. And she (Cristy) didn't mind that since she and Zack were in the same life science class, she sometimes had to deliver crumpled notes from Zack to Bess or Bess to Zack.

And Cristy (unlike Bess and Abby) didn't have to fake interest in Zack's soccer games, because she was a genuine fan. Not that Bess and Abby *bothered* to fake anything or even pretended to follow the game. When Cristy would forget herself and say something overly game-related or cheer or something, Bess and Abby would quickly hiss, "*Crisssty!* Cut it out! You're acting like a total geek."

But Cristy loved soccer and she probably would've really liked being on a team herself, but she never tried out or even brought up the subject because she knew Abby and Bess would laugh her right out of town.

Isn't it horrid what peer pressure can do? And Cristy's mom was so totally unathletic that it never even occurred to her to sign Cristy up for anything like that. So who knows, maybe Cristy would've been a famous, world-champion multimillionaire soccer star, on the cover of *Sports Illustrated,* if she weren't such a spineless wimp.

I suppose it's not too late. Maybe someday Cristy will

realize that Abby and Bess are *not* the rulers of the universe, and she'll grab a soccer ball and shin guards and have at it!

But for the time being, thanks to soccer, Cristy didn't mind Bess and Zack being boyfriend-girlfriend as much as she'd thought she would. And as far as her feelings about the whole Bess-stealing-Abby's-nonboyfriend thing, well, Cristy figured it this way: "If Abby's not making a big stink about it, who am I to gripe?" Plus, Cristy thought maybe the kind of crush Abby had on Zack was some *other* kind of boy-girl thing that wasn't necessarily related to boyfriend-girlfriend-ness. This last bit was pretty limp, but there you go.

Okay, that was Cristy. (Remember? We were doing our chapter THREE update on each girl?)

Now on to Bess. Bess still loved having a boyfriend. She especially loved it that everyone *knew* she had a boyfriend. And Zack was pretty nice most of the time, except that he kept handing her reams of totally lame poop-related jokes off the Net. He'd make Bess read every stupid word, page after stupid page, while he stood right there. And as if that weren't irritating enough, he'd then call her an "old stick" if she didn't laugh. Which was incredibly annoying, as I'm sure you can imagine, not to mention a seriously unromantic thing for a guy to call his girlfriend.

Example: Do we think Romeo called Juliet an old stick? We do not.

Abby is next, but what's there to say? She'd pushed her feelings down so deep that it was almost like not having them. She'd told herself these THREE things:

1) Zack didn't like *me* anyway. Bess couldn't really steal what was never mine in the first place, so it's not like Bess took him *away* from me, exactly.

2) Bess is one of my very best friends. And what kind of lousy cretin would let a *boy* (even one she's had a crush on for years) come between her and one of her best friends???

And 3) (THREE) No one should stand in the way of true love. They love each other. I'm happy for them. Period, end of discussion.

But to be *fair,* I have to report that Abby gave up wearing pajamas because the sight of Zack's name, passionately and unremovably carved inside her pajama drawer, was more than she could face before bed each night. She now slept in her mom's old T-shirts when she was at her mom's house, and her dad's at her dad's.

And while we are on the subject of *fairness,* I have one teeny thing to add. Remember I mentioned earlier the *remote* possibility that Bess had been suffering for who-knows-how-long with a crush on Zack that she'd kept secret (as long as she could) because she didn't want to hurt Abby's feelings? Well, I didn't mention the other two possibilities.

One is that Bess knew full well that getting Zack to be her boyfriend would tear Abby to shreds, but Bess either

1) didn't *care* if she hurt Abby, or 2) actually *enjoyed* hurting Abby. Which is worse? Either way it would have been Bess saying, "You can gouge Zack's name in all the furniture you want, loser, and it won't do you a bit of good. But if *I* so much as half-decide I think a guy is cute, I can have him with the snap of my fingers." Snap! (Fiendish, cackling laugh.)

Doesn't that give you shivers?

But if we believed Bess was truly evil, we'd just run in the opposite direction and tell Abby and Cristy and even Zack to run too, right? And since Bess is one of the THREE main characters, this story would be wrecked—which would be a shame, because when I stop writing this, I'll have no reason not to do all the chores I promised to do as soon as I'm done.

Plus, it would be wrong to leave Bess forever marked as the villain. Because number one: She's not. And number two: Cristy and Abby love her. And THREE: I do too, although not every single second of every day, and especially not when she borrows my stuff without asking, which I happen to think is *stealing*, not *borrowing*, don't you?

In fact, maybe she thought she was just borrowing *Zack!* Which leads us to the THIRD possible explanation for why Bess went after him: *Dumbness*. (Don't let her good grades fool you. There are smarts and there are *smarts*, and the two have nothing in common.)

Maybe since Bess had never had a long-lasting, name-carving, stuffed-animal-kissing, obsessive-type crush on a boy, she didn't understand what a big deal crushes like that can be to a girl. In other words, maybe she was just monumentally, certifiably, grade-A *clueless*.

True, she'd seen her own mom totally mangled by breakups and unreturned crushes. She'd even seen her big sister, Gilda, get slightly rattled by a dead-end relationship (although Gilda soon realized that she was way too good for the jerk and he was just too stupid for words).

But maybe Bess was so completely knuckleheaded that although she knew that *some* hearts get crushed by crushes, she didn't get it that *Abby's* heart would.

I'm wracking my brain, but I *can't* come up with a fourth explanation. Can you? Either Bess *knew* she was hurting Abby, or she didn't. Either she *cared,* or she didn't. Right? So the choices are that Bess was either 1) mean, 2) stupid, or 3) (THREE) the explanation that I mentioned in the first place about her having her own private crush on Zack for as long as or longer than Abby, like since preschool or birth. Which would mean that all her other crushes and boyfriends (including the high-drama romance with Max) were faked for cover.

Like anyone would even remotely buy *that*.

By the way, if you're waiting for *me* to tell you which is the right answer, you're wasting your time. I mean, I'm totally *flattered* that you think I'd know. And you're right that if I *did* know, I'd tell you for sure. But I'm shaking my head here, and that's the truth.

Mr. Wordsmith, my (fabulous) instructor in creative writing, says the important thing is to write about what *we know*. He said, "Don't write about the sea if you've never seen it." But even when we *are* writing about stuff we totally, totally know, inside out, it's pretty hard to really have a handle on *why* people do the things they do. So, there are things we narrators have to guess at—and other things we don't even dare guess. And I seriously don't think that should affect my grade in a bad way.

Maybe you're thinking I haven't done my research. Maybe you're wondering why I don't just *ask* Bess why she went for Zack. Well, the truth is, even asking a straight-out question doesn't always get a clear answer, and here's an example. When Bess first told her sister that Zack was her boyfriend, Gilda said: "But isn't that the guy Abby's all drooly over?"

Bess, flicking her hand as if to bat away such nonsense, answered, "That's a really *old* crush, like from third grade."

Gilda: "So?"

Bess: (getting defensive) "Well, it's like a tooth-fairy, Santa Claus, *baby* crush. It's not *serious*."

Gilda raised her eyebrows but didn't say a word.

Bess: (getting whiny) "And anyway, shouldn't there be a time limit on these things? I mean, if it doesn't click and the guy doesn't like you and anyone with a pea-brain can tell it's hopeless . . . like after a year or something . . . isn't it time to move on?"

Gilda raised her eyebrows a little higher.

Bess: (huffy) "And what's it to you, anyway?"

At which point Gilda dropped it. She was already late for work and her boss was repulsive enough without adding the extra repulsion of hearing him rant about how lazy and spoiled kids are today compared to the good old days of punctual hardworking cavemen like himself.

There's no teaching Bess anything anyway, in Gilda's opinion, so there you go.

Chapter THREE and a THIRD (part one)

lipstick

*Y*OU KNOW WHAT? I feel kind of guilty just going on like this, because remember back in chapter THREE when I said that the only symptom of Abby's feeling bad was that she couldn't face her pajama drawer? Well, that's not strictly true. I mean, it's not true that just sleeping in her parents' T-shirts took care of it and made her forget about Zack.

Some of Abby's Zack-thinking was a habit as hard to break as nail biting. Abby had to grit her teeth, or squeeze her eyes shut tight and shake her head, whenever her mind snuck Zack's face in place of the adoring actors in lovey-dovey commercials. It wasn't just commercials, either. Zack-attacks could occur without warning over the least thing.

Example: Abby and Bess and Cristy were going through the sale bin at Dora's Dazzle, when Bess pulled out a deep red lipstick and Abby's knees got instantly weak.

How many times had Abby secretly slathered on her mom's darkest red lipstick and, having written "Zack" on slips of paper, put kisses all over his name? Well, *how many* doesn't matter—this isn't about math. It's about a deep, sick sadness in the pit of Abby's gut. And if just the sight of a tube of lipstick could make her feel so awful, well, you can imagine.

Chapter THREE and a THIRD (part two)

men

NOW, WHERE WERE WE? Oh yeah—Saturday.

Well, unless it was pouring rain, Abby's mom went to garage sales early every Saturday morning. She called it "sailing" so people who didn't know her well would think she was athletic and outdoorsy. On the Saturdays when Abby and Spencer (and Wheezy) were with their mom, they sailed along with her. The rule was that they could buy anything they wanted for under five dollars. That promise is what kept them going, even on the mornings when they'd rather watch cartoons and vegetate like every other normal kid in America.

After garage-sailing they went to Flip's Flapjacks and ordered exactly the same thing every time from the same waitress (Nancy), who didn't even bring them menus anymore. Wheezy waited in the car for leftovers.

Anyway, *that* Saturday Abby found the coolest bracelet at the first port. (Get it? They *sail* into *port*?) The bracelet was kind of 1980ish and only cost a buck.

Spencer found a stuffed, dead baby alligator. Its mouth was sewn shut around its brown teeth. Yellow stuffing poked out of its ripped hide, and it was missing one glass eye, leaving a crusty, blank, dried-out eye socket.

"I need this," Spencer said.

Abby's mom shuddered. "Please no, Spency!"

"Eew, gross!" Abby said. "That's disgusting!"

Spencer hugged it closer and said, "Is not!"

"Is too!"

But the sticker on the dead alligator said $3.00 (THREE). And after all, an under-five-dollar promise is an under-five-dollar promise.

When they got to Flip's Flapjacks, Spencer unbuckled his alligator's seat belt and started hauling it out of the car, but Abby's mom said, "You absolutely may *not* bring that *thing* into the restaurant."

"But what if Wheezy eats him?" Spencer wailed.

Ick, that image practically killed Abby's appetite. Her mom turned a little green too. She opened the trunk and stood way, way back while Spencer locked his alligator in there.

Then the THREE of them went inside, and who do you

think was there, holding a booth for four? If you guessed Steve, you're right.

Here's a question for you: When she saw Steve crammed in a booth like a circus bear on a TRICYCLE, do you think Abby's first reaction was 1) miffed by his invasion of their sacred Saturday ritual, 2) confused in a nervous way, or 3) (THREE) glad?

Well, whichever you answered, you're right! Because Abby felt all those things at exactly the same instant. By the time she'd sopped her last bite of waffle in her last drop of syrup, though, she was leaning way more exclusively toward THREE (glad), because Steve had made her laugh so many times. Plus, it was funny that Nancy (their waitress) got so flustered by the shocking addition of Steve that she screwed up their order for the first time in forever.

After breakfast, Steve walked them to their car and Spencer showed him his alligator. Steve lit up like a (large) lamp and said, "Wow! I had a gator just like this when I was a kid! My uncle brought it from Florida. I bet my mom pitched it when I went to college. She always hated it."

Then Steve examined Spencer's rotting alligator corpse more closely and said, "Hey! Mine was missing the same eye! Isn't that amazing?"

Note: As you can imagine, Spencer was looking up (way, way up) at Steve like he was the hero of superheroes. And Abby's mom was too, because moms are total suckers for men who are nice to their kids. In fact, I bet I've even got *you* thinking Steve's a sweetheart, right? I mean, for Pete's sake, even *Wheezy* clearly adored Steve, and dogs are supposed to have a sense about these things.

Maybe you think I'm just setting you up to make a fool out of you later when Steve turns out to be a worm or worse. Don't you just hate it when you don't know who to trust and you feel like someone's messing with your mind? Well don't be so paranoid, because *I like Steve too!* I swear.

It was *Abby* who was suspicious of him. She remembered Bess saying that men *act* nice in the beginning. And she was thinking, Hmmmm, is Steve just pretending not to be grossed out by Spencer's hideous alligator? Will he dash back into Flip's Flapjacks to scrub the gator-cooties off his hands as soon as we drive away?

Abby stood by the car, watching her entire family from Mom to Wheezy practically batting their eyelashes at this gigantic stranger. And Abby had to admit that if Steve was acting, he was the best actor that ever lived. And she also had to admit (to herself) that if she wasn't careful, she'd soon be batting her eyelashes at him too.

Oh no! Did that mean that they were all being as lunk-headed about Steve as Lindy, Bess, and Gilda had been about (boo-hiss) Jonas? Were Abby and her family being totally tricked and bamboozled? Were they doomed to cry their eyes out later? Would Abby's mom gain thirty-six pounds and spend weeks in her ratty pajamas barely leaving her bedroom, like Lindy did after (boo-hiss) You-Know-Who?

Doesn't that thought make you shudder???

Dear Jonas,

In case you ever read this, I just want you to know that I totally hate your guts and think you are a reprehensible hunk of vomit and I hope you are very sick and broke and friend-less and hungry and lonely and miserable in every possible way, plus in unbearable pain. And I bet everyone who has ever met you agrees. So there.

Sincerely,
The Narrator

Chapter THREE
and Two THIRDS

soccer

IT TURNS OUT, in answer to Bess's earlier question of whether or not Zack was going to be the kind of boy-friend who came over, that he *would* have been, but he barely had time to sneeze, what with soccer (practice and games) and karate and clarinet (practice and lessons) and Hebrew school and homework. Therefore, theirs was mostly a school, telephone, and instant-messaging kind of romance.

So, to check him out, Bess's sister, Gilda, finally agreed to go to one of Zack's soccer games. But first she had a few errands to run, so she let Bess and Bess's friend Cristy tag along with her. Gilda couldn't stand *massive* doses of her little sister and her little sister's friends, but who could resist the occasional hour or two of total adoration? Cristy (who didn't have a big sister of her own) slavishly worshiped Gilda and hung on her every word.

Abby (who also idolized Gilda) couldn't go because she had cello lessons, but they all planned to meet at the soccer field. Pay attention now, because here comes a plot twist. Or maybe not a *twist* so much as a . . . well, I'm not exactly sure what you *call* this kind of thing, but it's more important than some of the other parts that I just went back and deleted.

It made me a little shaky to delete those entire conversations and scenes. Eliminating whole characters feels like being a murderer! I used to have a part in here about a guy named Fred and his mom and a longish thing about Fred's mom and her boyfriend Dr. Y, who was a bottom-feeding sleazeball, if you ask me. But I read it over and showed it to my writing teacher, Mr. Wordsmith, and we decided to take it out.

Actually, it was totally Mr. Wordsmith's idea to cut it. Maybe he's right, but I think Fred's mom and her pathetic relationship with Dr. Y were interesting *and* educational and fit well with this story's *theme,* which is basically, THE SEARCH FOR LOVE AND MEANINGFUL RELATIONSHIPS IN AMERICA TODAY. But once a thing is deleted, it's gone! Sigh.

Even though Fred's mom and her hopeless romance with Dr. Y are history, I still have every intention of telling you about Fred himself and his girlfriend, Emma, and even a tiny bit about Emma's best friend, Dawn—but not yet, because they aren't really in the story until chapter six. Although maybe now is actually as good a time as any to introduce them to you, because they (Fred, Emma, and even Dawn) were coming to this very same soccer game! The one that Gilda decided to attend so Bess would quit nagging her already.

Anyway, it wasn't a shocking coincidence that Fred was at the game, seeing as he's on Zack's team. You probably think I'm making this up just to stick the names *Fred* and *Emma* in here so they won't feel like total strangers later. But the truth is, Fred was the *goalie*!!! So of course he was there! And Emma came because she was Fred's girlfriend (although to tell the truth, this was only the second game she'd shown up for all season), and Dawn came along because she and Emma went practically everywhere together and there was nothing else to do, plus it was a gorgeous day.

But I'm getting ahead of myself here, because Emma and Dawn weren't at the game yet and neither were Cristy, Bess, or Gilda, although they would be soon. As a matter of fact, in just a little while the bleachers will fill up with fans without our really noticing, because we'll be much too busy watching Abby sweat bullets.

Now, here's the part where you've got to pay attention: Abby went straight from her lesson (cello) to the soccer field. Actually, to be scrupulously honest, Abby dropped her cello at her dad's house and *then* went straight to the field. Although, come to think of it, it was *two* hilltop fields edged all around by those extra-tall, extra-skinny palm trees (not the stumpy, shaggy kind) and an unbelievable view of the entire canyon. But I don't know why I bother describing the surroundings, considering Abby didn't notice *any* of it. What she *did* notice made her think she'd either gotten the time wrong or was at the wrong park, because a team of little tiny girls in red uniforms was there playing a team of tiny yellows. Great big hairy dads were bellowing their beards off on both sides.

Then Abby spotted Zack, way way over at the (nearly empty) far field, and here's what happened. But first, did I mention that Abby was early? The bleachers were still practically empty, except for a few parents who were sitting there reading the paper or sunning their upturned faces (although doctors tell us that's exactly how you get skin cancer).

Zack saw Abby coming and sprinted up to her.

When Abby's little eyes spied Zack running toward her, the old-habit thing kicked in: The oil on her forehead instantaneously spronged out into zits, so big, so red, so shiny, that they looked like headlights. And her heart went, Ker-*thump!* Ker-*thump!* Zack Alert! Zack Alert! He's heading this way!!!

Abby took a quick peek behind her (to see if he was running, smiling, waving to someone else). No one else was there! She smiled back at him, her lips curling up weirdly to hook on her braces. Mouth instantly desert dry, breath sour, pits oozing odorific oceans . . .

"Hey, Abbz," Zack panted, nearly out of breath. "Wanna

hit the *Cold Shoulder* after the game?" (Note: that's an ice cream, doughnut, frozen cappuccino place nearby.)

Abby, nearly blind with panic, could swear her eyelid was twitching like a psycho's. *"C-C-Cold S-Shoulder?"* she managed to stammer.

Zack nodded, running in place.

Abby was rooted to the field. Her legs and feet had turned to concrete. Zack pushed a particularly cute clump of hair out of his particularly cute eyes and said, "On Foothill?" Which is the name of a street. As if maybe poor stupid Abby didn't know what or where the *Cold Shoulder* was.

Abby mumbled some muddy reply that sounded like "Euxm doom mfab iegmeo," but it must've been clear enough to Zack, because he nodded and sprinted back toward his team.

Abby barely managed to clomp to the stands and hunch in a heap with her mind in a jumble, as you can imagine. If we tried to untangle each snarl of thought and put it in outline form, it would be something like this:

Strand 1) Wow! Zack likes me!

    1a) Wow! Zack asked me out!

    1b) Ick! I can't believe I stuttered like that!

Strand 2) Wow! Zack asked me out!

    2a) I can't believe how cute he looked running up to me with his hair all floppy in his eyes!

    2b) I acted like such an idiot!

Here's the sticky one:

Strand 3) (THREE) Wow!

3a) Wow!

3b) Totally *wow*!

Those last THREE wows kept Abby's brain very, very busy for however long it took the rest of Zack's team (and the other team) to arrive, warm up, arrange themselves on the field, and begin playing.

Now, one of my choices here, as your narrator, is to take Abby's mind apart, dissecting every fold of this new emotional *plot wrinkle*. I could get thermal and report it in terms of the temperature of Abby's sweaty, icy palms. Or I could describe it as art, discussing her skin color as she flushed, then paled, then flushed again—expressions flickering wildly, grin to grimace to grin.

But I don't think any of that is necessary, because what Abby was going through is so obvious and typical that it needs no explanation. I mean, if I'd said she strolled calmly to the bleachers, sat down, and took a lively interest in the game—who'd believe me?

So instead I'm asking you this: Do you think Abby got it right? *Did* Zack just ask her what she thought he asked her? Was this a *date*? And can you believe she was wearing that dorky green shirt with the stains all down the front??? It totally figures, doesn't it? See, that's why Lindy's life of careful grooming makes sense—because (this is useful advice!) you never know when you might suddenly wish you'd washed your hair and were looking hot.

Eventually, Gilda, Cristy, and Bess came along, chattering about nothing in particular until some fans yelled, "Down in front! For cryin' out loud!!!," making them plunk down (Bess on one side of Abby and Cristy on the other) giggling. Then Bess leaned across Abby and pointed Zack out to her sister. Gilda took one look at Zack and dubbed him Mini-Hunk, making Bess as proud as if she'd sculpted him herself. Abby went seasick green as one word flashed on her brain screen, and that word was *Bess!*

Oh. My. God, Abby thought. What do I tell Bess? And how do I meet Zack after the game without getting everyone all suspicious? And am I supposed to go *with* him to the *Cold Shoulder* or meet him there or what? And how am I going to ditch the girls without it being totally weird? Why didn't I ask these things when he was standing right there? I am such an idiot!!!

Abby seemed to remember there was a break in the game at some point. Was it like innings in softball? (She played in PE.) Or were there time-outs now and then when she could talk to him and clear up the details? How would she do *that*? How could she just walk up to him in front of everyone without it being entirely obvious?

Abby looked around. No way to pass him a note. She looked at the game. Zack was busy running around. She couldn't even get his attention to signal her distress or gesture in code.

Code? What code? She didn't know any code!

"You okay?" Cristy asked, noticing that Abby was twisting her face up, muttering to herself, and sweating even though it wasn't hot out.

Abby nodded, then said, "No." Turning as red as humanly possible without actually bursting into flame, she then shook her head and said, "I mean, yeah, I'm good. Hee-hee." Abby showed Cristy her teeth, hoping it made a convincing smile. But it didn't.

"What's the matter with you?" Cristy asked, getting alarmed.

Abby went deathly pale and answered, "Me? Nothing."

Then Cristy elbowed Gilda (who was sitting next to her) and said, "Abby's acting fishy. I think she's sick or something."

"Gross!" Bess said, scooting away.

Gilda leaned across Cristy's lap to put a comforting hand on Abby's arm. "I'm leaving in a little bit, Abbz. Want me to drop you at home?" she asked.

Think fast! Think fast! Abby told herself. Maybe this is good. I could hide out at home, put on some deodorant, change my shirt, then sneak back to the *Cold Shoulder* after the game. But how would Zack know that I haven't left for good? If I could catch his eye I could . . . what? Wink? Would that work?

Desperate times call for desperate measures, as they say. And Abby was perfectly willing to do just about anything, no matter how deranged, to keep this date with Zack. But she was absolutely *stumped*. There wasn't a single idea in her head. Not one.

Meanwhile, Gilda was getting ready to leave. She looked at Abby and said, "Well? What'll it be?"

Note: This is one of those moments when as your narrator, I've got some tricky decisions to make. You might think it's easy to just tell a story beginning to end, stick to the facts and that's that. But trust me, it's not that simple. For instance I could stop here and tell you what everyone else was thinking. But I have to decide if that would make reading this story a deeper, richer experience for you or if it would totally break the mood and get on your nerves. Should I spare you the suspense and cut to the end? Or should I tell you every gory detail and to heck with Abby's pride?

How 'bout half and half? Like this: Abby (winking frantically in Zack's direction) got up to leave with Gilda. If only he'd stop running after that idiotic ball for a second, she thought. But he didn't.

"Hope you feel better!" Cristy said in her concerned caretaker voice.

"Ditto," said Bess, shying away from possible stray germs.

Abby was too busy winking in the direction of the game to reply.

But once Gilda had led Abby to the car and Abby had closed the door and buckled her seat belt, she suddenly leaped up and said, "Wait! This'll screw it up totally!" And she popped her belt and grabbed the door handle.

"Huh?" Gilda asked.

Abby clamped her hand across her mouth.

Gilda looked at her watch. She had a date of her own

to get ready for. It was just a study date, and she wasn't sure if it was *her* or *her notes* that this guy Grant was interested in. And she wasn't exactly sure how interested she was in him either. But still, she needed a shower. However, one look at wild-eyed Abby told Gilda that her shower was o-u-t. She glanced at her watch and decided (with a deep inner sigh) that *unwashed* was okay, but *late* was not. So she'd give Abby THIRTEEN minutes, tops.

At least THREE of those minutes were spent swearing not to tell anyone, and the next THREE were spent promising not to laugh. You don't have to be a math genius to know that didn't leave much time for the storytelling *or* the advice-giving. But it didn't matter anyway, because after extracting Gilda's undying vow of secrecy till the grave, Abby's courage failed and she threw open the car door and bolted.

This left Gilda with THREE choices: 1) to give chase, 2) to pull the door closed, drive away, and forget it, or 3) (THREE) to sit still and wait right there in case Abby had a change of heart and returned. Gilda chose number THREE, natch, and consulted her watch. Ticktock. Ticktock. (Although it was digital and had neither ticked nor tocked in its life.)

Meanwhile, back at the bleachers, Bess was restless. The game was no duller than usual, but without Abby to talk to, it was pretty unbearable. Cristy was there, of course, but she was watching the game, which got on Bess's nerves and made her crabby on top of already being bored. She spied two girls from school (Dawn and Emma) and thought about going over to chat with them, but (like Cristy) they were concentrating on the stupid soccer game as if it were a steamy love scene in a movie.

What's *with* these people? Bess asked herself, getting more and more aggravated. When she couldn't stand it another second, she yanked Cristy to her feet and barked, "Let's go!"

Cristy blinked as if Bess had woken her up. "Go? Go where?"

"Who cares *where*?" Bess stamped her foot. "Anywhere but *here*!!!"

Cristy's eyeballs snuck back to the action on the soccer field, and she tried to sit back down, saying, "But the game—"

Bess gave Cristy's arm a sharp tug. "The *Cold Shoulder*," Bess said, knowing Cristy's weakness for sweets. "My treat," she added, knowing Cristy's double weakness for *free* sweets.

I've mentioned the *Cold Shoulder* by name and even put it in italics all those times before—so now you're supposed to gasp and say, "Uh-oh! Isn't that where Zack asked Abby to meet him???"

And now that you're worried about things getting messy, I'm going to end this chapter. That way you'll want to read the next one, right? (The narrator business is full of these sneaky little tricks.)

Chapter THREE
and Five Sixths

the imagined you

ARE YOU WONDERING where Abby bolted to? Well, Gilda was wondering too, but time was up. She'd already sacrificed her shower. And if she was going to be on time to meet Grant, she'd have to leave *right away*. So she did.

Cristy, meanwhile, was being half-dragged down the street toward the *Cold Shoulder*, when she suddenly felt a little nauseated in the gut and prickly around the forehead. "Ish," she said. "I think I'm getting what Abby's got."

(Hee-hee. *We* know that what Abby's got is a date with Zack, not stomach flu. But that's the fun of it: feeling smug and superior because we know stuff that the characters *wish* they knew!)

Now Bess was *really* exasperated. "I can't believe you'd get sick on such a gorgeous day! What is the matter with everyone?" But then she looked closer at Cristy, and her irritation turned to concern. (*She's not a beast, after all.*) Cristy really did look blotchy and strange.

"Eeew!" Bess said, recoiling. "You look horrible!" And she took Cristy firmly by the elbow, turned her right around, and gave her a shove toward home, saying, "Ick!"

Not really. She didn't abandon Cristy in her hour of need. The elbow grab was true, and the turning-around part, but then Bess walked Cristy all the way to her apartment building and even up the elevator to Cristy's door, muttering comforting words like, "You better not have given this bug to *me!*" (She was too sensitive to say out loud what was *really* on her mind, which, just between you and me, was: "Figures! Leave it to Abby and Cristy to gang up and die on me at exactly the same time!")

So, to review: Here we are at the top of chapter THREE and five sixths, with Abby who knows where, and Bess walking sick Cristy home, and Gilda heading off for a date with a guy named Grant (who turned out to be kind of funny in a too-cool-to-laugh-out-loud sort of way that made Gilda wish she'd brushed her teeth at least). He'd never read *The Little Prince* (she asked), but he didn't gag or act like he'd *refuse* to read it if someone lent him a copy. This info erased the thought of her little sister Bess's little friend Abby's mysterious disappearance from Gilda's brain. Completely.

And in case you're wondering, Bess abandoned her plan

to go to the *Cold Shoulder*, figuring it wouldn't be much fun all alone. Isn't that just like life? You go home and turn on the TV and veg away countless hours and brain cells while a perfectly juicy slice of life could be waiting for you right at the nearest ice cream joint? The scene! The drama! The outrage! The excitement of possibly walking in on your boyfriend, Zack, and one of your very best friends, Abby (supposedly home *sick!*), with their heads together, gazing into each other's eyes! Sharing a root-beer float with two straws!

But wait, no one was at the *Cold Shoulder* then except the two people who work there (one sweeping behind the counter, and the other talking to her grandma on the phone). The only customers were actually on their way out the door, and they consisted of one harried-looking mom and her three sticky-faced kids, one of whom was tantrumming over a dropped cone. Abby was nowhere to be seen, although soon, very soon, she was going to slip in the front door and go straight to the bathroom to pee and fluff her hair with nervous fingers.

Meanwhile, back on the field, Zack was finishing up the game and feeling darn good about himself because of THREE major assists and a splendidly executed goal. He looked over at the stands to make sure he was being admired, but discovered an empty bench where his adoring fans, Bess & Company, had been.

Which brings us to this crucial truth: Yes, Zack thought of them as *Bess & Company*. And like it or not, Zack had meant to meet *everyone* at the *Cold Shoulder,* not just Abby. His "you" (as in "Do *you* want to go to the *Cold Shoulder* with me?") was the plural you. The "you guys" you. Although actually there'd never actually been an actual *you.* Whether or not it was an *implied* you, it was an *imagined* you. To quote Zack exactly, he'd said, "Wanna hit the *Cold Shoulder* after the game?" (You can go back and check.)

(Reminder: We *all* do stupid things. We *all* misinterpret things from time to time, misread signals, have misunderstandings of one sort or another. *No one* is spared social embarrassment forever. So before you go laughing at Abby, remember this: You could be next!)

Zack shrugged at the empty benches and decided to go celebrate (they won) with Fred and some other guys from the team. Maybe Emma and Dawn too.

It turned out that everyone wanted pizza (not ice cream), and that sounded good to Zack too. So they all headed for Eddy's Eye-talian, which was in the exact opposite direction from the *Cold Shoulder,* where Abby sat (and sat and sat) straight-backed, trying to look calm while sweat tickled and itched down her body. Behind her (longish) bangs, her eyes flicked back and forth, watching the door and the clock, as her rocky road melted into rocky soup.

But let's not watch her squirm like a worm on the end of our hook. Let's resist the urge to go on and on about how slowly time crept by. And let's rise above the impulse to snicker about how, when Abby finally gave up, unstuck her sweaty thighs from the chair, and dragged her sorry self home—her dad grounded her. (She was supposed to have been home *hours* ago. And poor Spency had suffered such trauma over being abandoned that now he'll probably grow up even weirder than originally predicted. And never mind that while Spencer had been locked *outside,* Wheezy had been locked *inside,* leaving her no choice but to do her business under Dad's desk, again. One more doggy deposit and it was back to the inhumane society for ol' Wheezy. So Abby could have *that* on her conscience as well.) 'Nuff said.

Cristy called later that night to compare pukes, but Abby's dad said, "Abigail can't talk."

Cristy thought he meant Abby was too sick, which was more or less correct, although it wasn't the kind of sick that Cristy thought. Abby was the gut-twisting, hand-wringing, freak-outing kind of sick. The *what happened???* and *what should I do about it?* kind.

The next day Cristy felt better, but Abby felt worse and worse, wondering if Zack had stood her up on purpose or if he thought *she'd* stood *him* up by leaving. If *he* stood *her* up, or if he'd just been kidding when he asked her out, or *meant* to make a fool of her, then she'd have to bury herself alive under tons of humiliation and shame and mortification (although I think all THREE of those words mean the same thing).

On the other hand, if Zack thought *she* stood *him* up (by leaving the game early), thereby dissing and insulting and discouraging him from asking her out ever again, then she had to call him to explain. *Immediately!!!*

But here are THREE buts: 1) But she had no clue what to say. 2) But she was grounded from the phone. And 3) (THREE) But what about Bess? Shouldn't she be loyal to her friend, and honest and all that? Oh, and here's 4) But wouldn't it serve Bess right? A taste of her own medicine? Yes! Oops, a fifth but: 5) But wouldn't that make Abby just as bad as Bess? Yes again! (See the problem?)

Well now, seeing as you and I know that Zack had meant less than nothing by his *Cold Shoulder* suggestion, we want Abby to be denied phone privileges long enough to get her safely to the other side of this delusion so she never calls and embarrasses herself beyond recovery. In addition, it might help if she came down with the same bug Cristy had so she'd be too queazed out to defy her dad and call.

But no such luck. The pukiness she felt was strictly emotional and her dad forgot to tell her mom about the whole punishment-grounding thing, so when Abby (and Spencer and Wheezy) were pinged to Mom's house, the phone restriction was nulled.

Here goes.

Abby had been scripting, plotting, planning, practicing, and revising pretty much ever since leaving the *Cold Shoulder,* but when Zack's real live voice actually came through the tiny holes of the telephone, Abby started to babble. In spite of my full-disclosure, ultimate-honesty narration style, I think it would be just plain *cruel* of me to tell you how that conversation went. And that's not really censorship because (and here's the good news) Zack couldn't make heads or tails of what Abby was saying, so he doesn't know either. In fact, Abby was so unintelligible that he never really did get it that Abby thought he'd asked her on a date. He only knew that she was sorry about *something*.

Zack ended the conversation (if you can *call* it a conversation) by saying, "Well, Abbz, ask Bess to give me a call if you see her." Which told Abby all she really needed to hear: Bess was still the one who mattered, still the one he wanted to talk to, still Zack's girlfriend. Period, the end.

So, are you *disappointed* or *relieved* that it didn't turn out more humiliating for Abby? Never mind, don't answer that.

Chapter Four

the inevitable

THREE DAYS LATER Bess decided Zack was boring and broke up with him.

Perhaps you think that's that for the plot, since the Zack thing was pretty much the core of this story, and I don't blame you for thinking it, but you're totally wrong.

Chapter Five

various info-bits about pie and peppers, etc.

*Y*OU MAY FEEL that this chapter is beside the point, but this entire story is so pointy that just about *everything* is beside it. And so much happened while you were reading chapter four that if I don't quickly give you an update on the THREE moms' dating situations, you'll be left way behind.

We'll start with Lindy's (Bess's mom's) romance with the man Bess now thought of as Er-*ick* (although we all know that name-calling is sooo immature). Now that Bess had actually met him, she was entitled to her opinion, and her opinion was definitely Ick. Or to be more exact: "Ick, puke, ick, vomit, ick!" And her sister, Gilda, totally agreed.

The cows were still cowering behind the couch, and

tasteless twigs and gravel seemed to have replaced every edible crumb in the apartment. Now everyone had to leave their shoes at the front door when they came in, although no one explained to Bess or Gilda why shoes indoors were a spiritual no-no. And Bess suspected that Er-*ick* had hypnotized her mom, because Lindy now spent a ridiculous amount of time *chanting.*

Bess would hear her mom's voice and she'd call out, "I'm in here!" But Lindy's reply would be muffled, making Bess yell, "*What?*" several times louder. But *still* unable to make out what Lindy was saying, Bess would hang up on Cristy or Abby (often midsentence) to go hunt through the apartment, calling, "Yoo-hoo! Lindy?" Until she'd find her mom perched unnaturally somewhere, endlessly repeating a phrase that sounded like infant baby babble. This happened more times than you'd believe and was, of course, Er-*ick*'s great idea.

The next dating update is on Abby's mom, who had been seen kissing Steve on two separate occasions. The first one was a peck on the cheek in the kitchen. Abby's little brother, Spencer, caught it and said, "Yuck!" But to tell the truth, Abby hadn't been all that grossed out.

The second one was at the beach and this one was an all-out *smooch!* I'll tell you about it quickly, then we'll get right back to our story. I promise.

Beach Scene: Spencer cheered when Abby's mom told them they were going to the beach the next day with Steve. Deep in her secret brain cells Abby was a tiny bit relieved too, because Steve hadn't been around for a while and she'd been kind of wondering why.

But first things first. Abby asked, "Can Bess and Cristy come?"

And her mom said, "No."

They went back and forth awhile with Abby saying "Pretty please?" and her mom saying "No." Until Spencer muttered, "Do you think Steve wears trunks or a Speedo or what?" It stopped Abby dead in her tracks to picture such a thing.

But the next day was too cold and windy for any kind of swimsuit. They climbed the rocks and poked around in the tide pools, glad to be wearing clothes because the wind was stinging with sand. Nonetheless they spread a blanket and set up their picnic. Steve had brought the food—deli stuff, sandwiches, and pickles, and doggy treats for Wheezy. As Steve opened the thingie of potato salad, he said, "No bell peppers, Abby."

Wow! Can you believe he'd remembered that she hated green peppers? (Please take a second here to appreciate that.) Even Abby's *mother* forgot half the time and put peppers in things, or ordered them on their pizza. So I ask you, How can you *not* love a guy like that?

Abby was stunned into silence and shoveled in the pepper-free potato salad until her ribs ached. Then the wind picked up one, two, THREE paper napkins and blew them away. Abby and Spence jumped up to chase them, but while Abby kept after the napkins, Spence and Wheezy veered off after some seagulls.

That's when Abby turned around to yell something back to her mom and saw the smooch. It made Abby feel weird, as you can imagine. Good, bad . . . weird.

Now, to complete the mom update, Cristy's mother was still hanging out alone, but she didn't seem to mind a bit. And *something* had to stay the same, right?

The girls had thought about fixing Cristy's mom up with Bess's dad so Bess and Cristy could be sisters and every night of their lives would be a sleep-over party. But actually picturing Bess's dad trying to squish into Cristy's mom's apartment cracked everyone up. There wasn't enough room for him. Not because of his fat. There seemed to be no shortage of women who liked him and were willing to overlook his gut. They probably didn't know that he (Bess and Gilda's dad) had never bothered to read his oldest daughter's favorite book even though she'd bought him a copy with her own money and it was *right there* on the shelf in front of him and would take maybe two hours tops to read and that's if he was practically reading backwards.

But (speaking of books) the *real* reason Bess's dad couldn't move in with Cristy's mom (besides the fact that 1) he had no interest in doing so, and 2) he happily lived and worked in Farmington Hills, Michigan) was that he had tons of *stuff,* like pool tables and entertainment centers and treadmills and his ancient Tibetan sculpture collections, plus his THREE cars, not counting his motor-cycle. And although one car was technically a dune buggy, it would still need a parking space and Cristy's mom's apartment building only allowed her one little off-street parking space, period.

Plus, I just can't picture entertainment centers and treadmills fitting Cristy's mom's decor. Her place was decorated completely in books. They were piled on every surface, lying open on the kitchen counter, stacked on the floor, on tables, and next to the toilet. Bookshelves loomed, threatening to topple, in the front hall. And you should've seen Cristy's mom's bedroom! Her bed was so heaped with books (and cats and pillows) that I've no idea how she squeezed in there to sleep.

The real danger, though, would be that if Bess's dad and Cristy's mom fell in love, he'd take her back to Farmington Hills, Michigan, with him, dragging Bess and her sister, Gilda, along! Neither girl was one bit interested in moving to Farmington Hills, Michigan, where the winters get so cold that your lips crack and bleed when you smile! Brrrr! Forget it!

Whoa!!! This chapter was *not* supposed to be about home decorating or chapped lips. We were talking about fixing the girls' stray parents up into tidy bundles so the girls could be sisters. And in case you're wondering why the THREE friends considered making *Bess* and Cristy sisters but not *Abby*, the reason is that it was clearly hopeless. Abby's dad and Cristy's mom had already known each other forever and no one had ever seen even the teeniest sparks fly between them. Plus Abby's dad was deathly allergic to cats and Cristy's mom loved her kitties way more than she liked most humans.

And I suspect that Abby wouldn't have been gung-ho for her mom to marry Bess's dad either, not only because that was back when her crush on Zack was pure and un-challenged and she'd have rather torn her eyes out than move away from him. (To Farmington Hills, Michigan, remember?) But also because (as Gilda overheard Abby whisper to Cristy at Bess's birthday party almost THREE years ago) she (Abby) secretly thought Bess's dad was a little on the slimy side.

Gilda's revenge for this insult to her father had been to give Abby and Cristy slices of birthday cake with parts of the word *Happy* on them instead of frosting flowers. This was ironic since both girls were desperately *un*happy, as well as confused, since there were still flowers left uncut on the cake! Neither girl had *any* idea why Gilda was being so mean, and they couldn't have been more miserable.

In fact, *misery* was pretty much the party theme that year. Never mind the clubbing incident with the piñata stick that left a huge welt on one party guest's noggin. And forget the mysterious disappearance of all the party favors. The real question is, Why was it *Gilda's* job to slice and serve birthday cake to a bunch of whiny brats? Where were the *adults*, for Pete's sake?

Well, to be fair, Lindy *wanted* to help, but that was when she was so miserable (there's that word again!) over (boo-hiss) Jonas that Gilda didn't trust her with the knife!

And Bess and Gilda's dad was busy making goo-goo eyes at the date he'd brought all the way from Farmington Hills, Michigan (without warning).

Maybe you're wondering if bringing a date to his little girl's birthday party and cootchie-cooing her in front of everyone *was* in fact a bit slimy (as Abby had suggested). And that's a perfectly reasonable question, which is why Gilda gave Abby and Cristy inferior pieces of cake instead of, say, giving them *no* cake, or mashing the cake in their faces.

But other than that one little time (as far as I know), Abby and Cristy kept mum on the subject of Bess's dad because everyone knows that people aren't allowed to say bad stuff about any kid's dad, besides that kid, period, the end, unless they're positively positive that no one can hear them. But the fact remains, as I said before, that I'm pretty sure Abby wouldn't want her mom to marry him.

The whole *sister* idea stunk anyway, because unless Abby's mom married Bess's dad and Cristy's mom married Abby's dad (which would be way too much fixing up to fix up), someone would've been totally left out. And anyway, Bess, for one, already *had* a sister (Gilda) who (I'm just guessing here) probably didn't particularly want another little sister poking through her things, being annoying in the car, using her hair dryer, hogging the bathroom, and so on.

Plus, if things kept going the way they looked like they were headed with Steve, Abby might have to drop out of the D of D anyway. Well, no, she'd still be a daughter of divorce even if her mom got remarried, so forget I said that. And while you're forgetting, forget the other thing too (about Bess's dad being a slime) because he's *really* not, he just gives that impression. And I'm sure that if he *truly* understood how much *The Little Prince* meant to Gilda, his eldest daughter, he'd take the time to read it.

Phew! We're done with the update. See? I *told* you you'd missed a lot back there. Now if you don't mind, can we get back to the story?

Okay, so about a week after Bess broke up with Zack, she called Abby and said, "Lindy's roots are showing."

Abby said, "Huh?"

"My mom. Her roots. The orange is growing out and you can see the brown hair underneath!"

"So?" Abby asked, because she was distracted by something Steve was doing.

"*So???*" Bess howled. "I'm telling you Lindy's roots are showing and you say '*So*'?"

Abby turned her back on Steve and made herself pay closer attention to her friend. "What do you want me to say, Bess?"

"I don't *want* you to say anything. It's just that roots mean trouble. I bet Er-*ick* is breaking up with her!"

And all Abby could think was, I hope Steve doesn't break up with *my* mom. But what she *said* was, "I've gotta call you later, 'kay?"

In case you wondered what Steve was doing that was so distracting, it was this: He'd come in with four pink bakery boxes dwarfed in his giant hands. In each box was a pie.

Why pie? Because a few days ago, at the windy picnic on the beach, Steve had told them that he'd won a pie-eating contest when he was in college. Spencer and Abby thought that sounded like a blast.

Abby's mom wasn't thrilled with the idea, but here was Steve with a pie for each of them.

When Abby got off the phone, Steve held up a gigantic finger and said, "The rules: Number one, no hands. You've got to get down there and eat face-first like a dog."

Spencer giggled uncontrollably.

Mom sighed.

"Two." Steve raised a second finger. "Whoever scarfs up their entire pie first wins! Ready?"

By the time Abby was globbed with blueberry filling from eyebrows to neck, with a piece of crust mysteriously wedged in her ear, she was laughing way too hard to remember Bess's call about Lindy's roots. So she didn't call her back.

Chapter Five and a THIRD

a note about Lindy's roots (and a confession)

BESS'S MOM, LINDY, took her personal grooming *very seriously*. She spent a large percentage of her income (from her job as an assistant interior designer) on the beautification of her *self*, including: lotions, gels, paints, sprays, masks, and scents for *home* improvement of hair, nails, and skin, and professional outside assistance such as her beautician, manicurist, waxer, and personal Pilates trainer. Plus clothing, of course, and accessories. (An assistant interior designer can't exactly show up like a total slob and expect to keep clients, now, can she???)

That isn't to say that Lindy was shallow, because she wasn't. And I'm not just saying that so she won't get mad if she reads this. (Maybe you've noticed I'm going for *full truth,* except for names. And I hope you appreciate it, because I may very well end up alone, shunned and despised as a result of all this honesty.)

And, as I mentioned earlier, this obsessive good-grooming thing comes in handy if you happen to meet a cute boy when you're not expecting to, such as when Gilda wished she'd washed her hair for that study date with Grant before he turned out to be a little *too* cool for her taste. Meaning he was too cool and laid-back to remember to be where he'd said he'd be when he said he'd be there. THREE tastes of that and Gilda no longer gave the least fig whether her hair was clean for Grant, but the point is, Lindy's hair, makeup, etc. wasn't as silly as some may think.

Oh wait. The *real* point is that although Lindy was not a vain or superficial woman, neither was she the type to simply *lose track* of her hair color. No, Lindy wouldn't *forget* to touch up her roots. Nor would an appointment with her hairdresser normally slip her mind, unless something was definitely *not* okay.

And now, the confession: There's something I didn't tell you about the beach scene with Steve. At the time, I thought I had a good reason for skipping this part, but now I realize it's best to just give over the whole, entire, complete, uncensored, unabridged story—and so what if it sounds a little over the top? What I mean is, I was afraid that if I put in this last bit, you'd think I'd crossed the line and gone too far in the direction of corny, hearts and flowers—the direction that would make you lose all faith in me. But now I realize that schmaltzy, sappy stuff is part of reality too. And like it or not, sometimes reality *is* hokey. We always hear about "harsh, cold reality," but warm baby bunnies, fluffy kittens, and chubby puppies are real too, right?

Anyway, what I'm trying to say is this: Remember how Abby's mom's "friend" Steve knew that bell peppers made Abby burp and reburp that sick green taste for hours and hours till she'd want to scream? Well, maybe Steve didn't know *that* exactly, but he *did* remember that she'd plucked them out of her Chinese food, which is more than practically anyone else. For instance, what do you think the chances are that Cristy or Bess remember Abby's *anti*-bell-pepper feelings?

Not that close friends, perfect in every other way, don't forget these things about each other. They totally do. For instance, Abby's favorite candy is Baby Ruth, so that's the kind she buys. Heaven knows Abby would be happy to eat the whole candy bar herself, but she always offers to share with her friends, forgetting that the least taste of peanut could very possibly send Cristy into anaphylactic shock, which is a *very* bad thing to be sent into, as I'm sure you can imagine.

But the point here has nothing whatever to do with peanuts or even bell peppers. The point is . . . Shoot! Now I've completely lost my train of thought. I *hate* that. I totally hate that! Don't you? It's because all that talk of peanuts and candy got me all hungry and sidetracked. Anyway, let's just pause for a little snack here. It'll come back to me later, maybe.

No, wait, there's something *else* I bet you've been wondering about. How was Bess feeling about the breakup? Actually, you're probably wondering what *Abby* was thinking and feeling about it too, but let's do Bess first, because she was the one whose relationship actually broke. Or maybe you're *not* wondering how Bess was doing, figuring that since she's the one who did the breaking, she was probably fine.

Well, I'm not saying Bess *wasn't* fine. It's just that people aren't *necessarily* fine just because they are the up-breakers, or because they *say* they are. Although it's often crystal clear to both people who is doing the breaking and who is getting broke, it's not always. If one of them is saying, "No, please don't leave me! I'll try hard to be better, I swear!" then *that* person is probably *not* the one whose idea it was to break up.

But lots of times people *say* they were the one who ended a relationship when they weren't. And other times people say that it was *mutual* and that both are happy with the decision to just be *friends,* when really, he (or she) calls his (or her) house six dozen times between midnight and four a.m., shrieking and weeping. Or hangs around his (or her) locker or house, pretending he/she is "just passing by." Or leaving apologizing/angry notes under his/her door. And/or bugging his/her friends and relatives, and generally disgracing him-/herself in every imaginable way.

So now the guy (or girl) whose idea it was to split up has quickly gone from thinking that the ex just wasn't right for him/her, to thinking he/she is a dangerous lunatic. Now he/she is tempted to call the police and move to a new city and take on a whole new identity just to avoid him/her.

Note: The whole he/she, him/her business can be so annoying. I'm surprised more narrators don't choose to write about *its*, like carrots or lamp shades.

Anyway, just to prove how tricky breakups can be (as far as who does what to whom), let's say *Person Number One* says, "I hate everything you do and say. I hate your clothes, your voice, your looks, your smell, your taste in music, your politics, your family, your furniture, your pets, and your breath." And *Person Number Two* replies, "Then I never want to see you again!" Who (in that case) would you say broke up with whom?

Just like with broken bones there are hairline fractures and multiple fractures, and some need to be set with anesthetic and sterilized pins in an operating room by surgeons in unflattering disposable outfits with matching paper shower caps—and they just slap a cast on the others.

Well . . . Bess and Zack's break went *exactly* like this: Zack shoved a batch of jokes under Bess's nose and she said, "Ya know what? I hate these stupid things. And I'm sick to death of you giving them to me."

And he said, "But they're funny!"

And she said, "No, they're *not* funny, they're dumb and I hate them."

And he said, "*Gaaad,* what's the matter with *you* today?"

And she said, "It's not just today, it's every day. I've *always* hated your stupid jokes, as anyone with half a brain would've *noticed* by now, if they weren't a total pig-head!"

And Zack said, "Who you calling pig-headed?"

And Bess said, "Well, du-uh."

"Are *you* calling *me* dumb?" Zack asked incredulously. "*You,* who can't even remember your locker combination, are calling *me* of advanced placement English *and* math, *dumb*???"

Bess nodded, so Zack said, "Fine!"

And Bess said, "Fine!" And that was that.

But when Bess got home from school, she felt bad. Not because she didn't think Zack and his jokes were dumb, because she did. And not because she wanted him back as her boyfriend, because she didn't. No, Bess felt bad not for herself, but for Zack. She figured he was probably all glum and depressed, maybe even suicidal, because he'd loved her and she was so un-get-over-able (if that's a word).

Bess decided she'd better call Zack and make sure he was okay. She felt it was the least she could do to offer sympathy for the pain she'd caused.

Her sister, Gilda, thought this was cruelty masking as kindness—that Bess just wanted to watch him bleed and see for herself how powerful she was (like a criminal returning to the scene of the crime). But Gilda didn't have a chance to say this, because Bess was already dialing Zack's number. Gilda only had time to mutter, "Leave the kid alone, you conceited little . . ."

Until shhh, listen: Ring! Ring! Zack picked up the phone and said, "Hey," meaning hello.

Bess replied, "Zack? You okay?"

And he said, "What's it to *you*?"

And she, thinking he was trying to act brave while his heart was aching, said (in her most drippingly sympathetic voice), "I just need to know that you'll be all right, Zachary."

And he actually *chuckled* and said, "Get over yourself, Bess. *I* did." And he hung up *laughing*!

Eew! Can you imagine??? How insulting! And *em-bar-rass-ing*!!

Not as bad as the Max thing at least (which I know you want to know about, but as far as poor Bess is concerned, *way* too many people know already, and one embarrassment at a time is plenty). Luckily no one knew about *this* phone call except for Bess and Zack. And (through no fault of her own) Bess's sister, Gilda, who was standing right there and couldn't help but overhear.

Chapter Five and a Half

inserted against my better judgment

IT OCCURS TO ME that Abby and Bess are getting way bigger parts in this story than Cristy, who is an equally important point in the TRIANGLE. Well, actually, it occurred to Mr. Wordsmith when he read my rough draft. And maybe he's right that Cristy needs a few more lines, although I personally think not.

When the famous novelist Amy Goldman Koss came to our class and gave a talk, one of the many interesting things she said was that writing the *first* draft is a terrific blast and loads of fun: "a fast and furious brain dump!" (her words, not mine). But rewriting is where she earns her money. "That's when it's *work*," she said. I guess giving Cristy more lines is the sort of thing she meant.

So, in case Mr. Wordsmith is right, let's look in on

Cristy and her mom that same evening: Their heads are propped on pillows at either end of the living room hammock, each with her nose in a book. Two cats sleep amid the tangle of mother-daughter toes. A kitten bats playfully at a waving tassel as the hammock gently rocks. We see Cristy's brow furrow. She marks her place with the yellow satin bookmark that has been handed down, mother to daughter, for THREE generations, and she says, "Excuse me, Momma."

"Yes, dear?" Ms. Levine answers. (Shoot. It totally wrecks my cozy scene that I don't know her first name! But you get the picture, right? They are calm and close and about to have one of those bonding, heart-to-heart, mother-daughter chats that make us all weepy on Mother's Day wishing we had that kind of chat with our own mothers.)

Anyway, "Yes, dear?" Cristy's mom answers, closing her book and looking up. (Note: She did *not* say, "Wait a sec. Sheesh, can't you see I'm *busy*???" Nor did she grunt and ignore.)

"Momma, there's weird stuff going on with Abby and Bess."

Then Cristy's mom replies with something encouraging and sympathetic and trustworthy, and Cristy says, "It's the boy thing."

Cristy's mom nods understandingly . . .

Ish. I hate writing this kind of scene. And I'm positive

that this story doesn't need more Cristy scenes. You totally *get* her, don't you?

(Note to Mr. Wordsmith: There's always the THIRD draft if you *still* think Cristy's being cheated. But maybe we just need a review!)

.

REVIEW:

1) Cristy was not a leader type but she was a good friend and loyal follower and everyone totally loved her to pieces.

2) Cristy was not a rocket scientist, but no one ever accused her of being a box of rocks either.

3) (THREE) Cristy always meant well.

P.S. She was terribly allergic to peanuts.

Okay? Better? Can we go on with the story now???

Chapter Five and Two THIRDs

the THREE little pigs

*W*ant to know who won the pie-eating contest? Well, Steve did, natch. He's only like ninety times the size of everyone else. But I'll tell you how it went.

I mentioned earlier that the reason Abby forgot to call Bess back about Lindy's roots was that Abby was busy laughing her head off. A head, I might add, that was pretty nearly covered in gloppy blueberry-pie filling. She'd managed to chow down almost a THIRD of her pie! Her mom had dropped out of the contest before her, having eaten the equivalent of a puny half slice.

It may sound sexist that the females caved first, but what can I say? The truth is unalterably the truth, right?

Meanwhile Spencer, age six, weighing in at forty-THREE pounds maximum, was going head to head in the ring with Steve at a lumbering two hundred and THIRTY-THREE.

Both were giving it their all until Steve raised his big, gooey face and yelled, "I win!" And sure enough, his pie plate was practically clean. Little Spencer kept at it, willing to die, it seemed, for the second-place title.

"Hey, Spency, that's enough," Abby's mom said after a while. Then a few seconds later, "All right, Spence, time to quit!" But you guessed it, on he chomped.

"Spencer Falzetta! Stop right this second!" Abby's mom said, getting stern. But he ignored her until she grabbed his little shoulders and yanked his face out of the pie plate. That was not a wonderful moment. But on careful examination of the remains of the four pies, it *did* in fact turn out (to the best of anyone's ability to judge) that Spence could in fact legitimately claim the *runner-up* title. He was thrilled out of his gourd.

From there Spencer was marched off for a bath, leaving Abby and Steve in the kitchen to clean up. They'd never been alone before, but considering the pie thing, it would be practically *impossible* to go back to being shy. So they chatted away, giggling about Abby's one brother (Spence) and Steve's four brothers (Groucho, Harpo, Zeppo, and Chico).

After that, Abby went to bed and to sleep until THREE a.m., when she woke to the sound of bombastic barfing. It was Spencer turning inside out. Her mom was with him. Abby fought her own gag reflex and stumbled half asleep into the kitchen for a drink of water. Steve was still sitting at the kitchen table. That was a surprise.

"You okay?" Steve asked, looking hangdog.

Abby nodded sleepily. "Thirsty," she said.

"I'm sorry," he said. "That was a terrible idea. A really terrible idea. I never should've brought those pies. What was I thinking?"

Abby got her drink and tried to make sense of what Steve was saying.

He looked over at her. "I really apologize," he said.

Abby nodded and mumbled something like, "It was fun," and shuffled off to bed.

In the morning Steve was gone and Abby forgot the whole groggy scene until she caught the unmistakable whiff (eew) of vomit in the bathroom. Then it occurred to her to worry that Steve might feel *so* guilty about pie-poisoning Spencer that he'd never be able to face him or her or their mom ever again.

Chapter Six

meanwhile

*A*bby, Bess, and Cristy had two emergency girl-friends—not the kind you call fifty times a night, but the kind you eat lunch with when your best friends are absent or you're fighting with them. I mentioned these girls before, remember? In an attempt to *foreshadow*. So, if you've been paying attention and taking notes, you know that they are (D) Dawn and (E) Emma. (Note: They were at the soccer match where Abby thought Zack had asked her to go to the *Cold Shoulder*, which out of habit I'm still putting in italics.)

Stop! What a perfect time to tell you about Dawn's mom! Maybe Mr. Wordsmith will think Dawn's mom is too *outside* to be mentioned here, but I respectfully disagree for THREE reasons (although I can only think of two right this second). 1) Dawn's name just came up naturally in the story, so it's not *that* weird to be suddenly talking about her mom. And 2) Dawn's mom's story is conveniently similar to the Bess and Emma story I'm about to tell you. And to the Bess-Zack-Abby story that started the whole thing.

See, Dawn's best friend, Emma, had a boyfriend named Fred (F). (Remember? The goalie?) And not long after Bess dumped Zack, Cristy told Abby that Bess had told her that she (Bess) thought Fred (Emma's boyfriend) was a hoot. To be exact, what Cristy said was, ". . . Bess thinks Fred is so funny. I think he's a jerk."

Let me back up. Abby and Cristy had just dropped Bess at the computer lab, and they were heading toward their classroom. (Their class has to divide up and take turns using the computers because their district keeps voting down tax increases for public education since all the rich people's kids go to private schools, which cost buckets of money, so they don't want to fork over still *more* dough for other people's kids. And who can blame them? Plus rich people often figure that money is totally wasted on poor people because if they *really* appreciated it, they'd *have* some. And if they *really* valued education, they wouldn't send their kids to such overcrowded schools that don't even have enough computers to go around. Not that I have anything against rich people, because I totally don't. In fact, I have every intention of becoming one myself someday, and the sooner the better.)

Anyway, Abby and Cristy (after dropping Bess at computer lab) were heading down the hall when they saw Dawn and Emma. They were about to wave and say hi, when Fred suddenly barreled past and slam-dunked his math book over Dawn's head, into Emma's locker, knocking stuff over with a chaotic, metallic *clang* that jolted Emma and Dawn into screaming as loud as they could.

Whatever Abby and Cristy had been talking about was lost forever, and instead Cristy said, "I have no idea why Bess thinks Fred is so funny. I think he's a jerk." Try to remember that. Actually, I'll repeat the important part: Cristy said, "Blah blah . . . (quote) Bess thinks Fred is so funny (unquote) . . . blah." Okay, hold that thought while I quickly tell you about Dawn's mom and aunt.

Dawn's mom is a sweet, friendly person named Kim who has a sister named Sheila. (Notice there are no adjectives such as "sweet" anywhere near Sheila's name.) When they were younger, Sheila stole away every single boy that Kim liked, leaving her in perpetual tears.

Over the years, Sheila branched out and took boyfriends (and still later, husbands) away from other people besides her sister. When sweet Kim was marrying her very own sweet husband (Dawn's dad), she was practically afraid to invite her own sister to the wedding!

For the record, though, you should know that sweet, friendly Kim is now living a wonderful life of pure happiness (still married to Dawn's dad, making her possibly the *only* undivorced woman over the age of sixteen in this entire story), and Sheila grew up to be a miserable old toad.

(Oh. Maybe I should change *their* names too. Remind me to go back later and call them Beila and Fim, but I don't have time now because I have a story to tell, remember?)

But wait a second. We'll get back to what Cristy told Abby that Bess said about Fred after I mention that there are *all* kinds of Sheilas—meaning people who don't like to make their own decisions. Not only do they prefer pretested and preselected boyfriends, but same for their books and movies (reviewed) and fashions (imitated).

I'm just guessing here, but I wouldn't be a bit surprised if *little* sisters were more likely to be Sheila-types than olders or onlys, seeing as little sisters are always hovering jealously in their big sisters' shadows.

On second thought, I myself am an *older* sister, and yet I almost always wish I could swap my meal in a restaurant for whatever the person with me was served. The other person's order *always* looks better.

Nonetheless, if I were Gilda, say, and my little sister pulled a stunt on me like Sheila did on Kim, I'd set her straight in a heartbeat. She could just kiss her CD collection and everything else she held dear good-bye. Including Bun-Bun, and I'm totally not kidding.

But the relevant question is whether Bess was going to be like Dawn's aunt Sheila *forever* or if it was just a nasty one-time fluke when she went after Zack. Would Bess snap out of it and return to being the kind of friend Abby and Cristy could safely confess their crushes to without making Bess zero in on the boys in question? More to the point: Was the "Fred is so funny!" comment harmless? (Aren't these questions mysterious and perplexing food for thought?)

Okay, now you can forget all about Beila and Fim. They weren't even in alphabetical order, which shows what minor characters they were. And as for Fim's daughter, Dawn, although she has truly remarkable golden-retriever-colored hair, which I totally envy, she really doesn't have much of a part in this story either. Emma and her boyfriend, Fred, do, though. From here on in, they are practically almost *main* characters, although not really.

Anyway we aren't sure what made Bess think Emma's boyfriend, Fred, was so funny. It might have been the way he pretended to trip over things that weren't there, but Bess had seen him trip countless times before, so who knows? And Cristy didn't tell Abby what made her (Cristy) think that Bess thought Fred was funny. Abby wondered if Bess had said something about Fred out of the blue. Had they been talking about the relative funniness of boys in their grade? Or had they been discussing boys with *F* names or what?

That's often the problem with gossip. Things get repeated in bits and pieces, out of context, missing the big picture. That is why I personally try very hard to give you all the related background scoop on everything. I hope you appreciate it.

I suppose there are those who'd say that Cristy had no business telling Abby what Bess had said about Fred. But unless Bess *specifically* said something to Cristy like, "Don't tell anyone, but confidentially, I think Fred is *sooo* funny," then Cristy was under no real obligation to keep what Bess said a secret. Do the antigossip police think we should never talk about anyone *ever*? Can you imagine a more boring or pointless existence than that?

In any case, Abby squinted at Cristy there in the school corridor while Emma and Dawn continued to scream and Fred apologized (loudly) for knocking everything out of Emma's locker. And here's what Abby thought to herself (as she squinted): Something about this seems familiar.

Then, fifteen minutes later in class: *Bingo!* The pieces fit and Abby thought, Bess is going after *Fred*!!!

Note: I'm tempted to remind you that Abby *never said anything* to anyone about how she felt about Bess going after Zack. And the reason I'm tempted to remind you is because that fact is *enormously* important for understanding the upcoming *plot twist*. But I'll assume you haven't forgotten and I'll just go on to say this: After school, between her hip-hop lessons and her orthodontist appointment where she got blue spacers, Abby thought again about the Fred and Emma versus Bess situation, and said to herself, "Poor Emma's too dumb to know she's in danger!"

Abby probably pictured Emma and Fred suspended in a delicate, twinkly bubble, holding hands and gazing sweetly into each other's eyes with little red hearts popping around them. That's how she used to picture herself and Zack before Bess came along and . . . well, you know.

During her hip-hop class (when she was supposed to be concentrating on her hip and her hop), Abby thought, I have to stop Bess! So when she got home to her dad's, she marched right to the phone and called.

Here's the complete transcript of that call, word for word, as accurate as any court report. Abby said, "Bess home?" And Bess's sister, Gilda, replied, "No."

That wasn't what you'd call exemplary telephone etiquette, but in the interest of truth, we'll let the quotes stand. As far as I know, no one blames anyone for Abby's bad manners, but Gilda's dad blames her mom (his ex-wife) Lindy's sloppy parenting skills for Gilda's. Lindy, in turn, blames *his* gene pool. When she thinks the girls are out of earshot, Lindy refers to her ex-in-laws (now out-laws) as a family of pigs. And Gilda once saw Lindy push her nose up with her finger and whisper "Oink! Oink!" behind her husband's back when they were still married. That sort of thing scars a child for life, you know, and may very well be why Gilda is doing so badly in geometry.

Oops! Here I am going into microscopic detail about *this* (ill-mannered) THREE-word phone call, when I completely flaked on the *way* longer and infinitely more crucial conversation back when Abby found out that Bess and Zack had broken up!

That bit should've probably been stuck in back around chapter four and a THIRD! But we're here now, so let's just act casual and whistle on to the next chapter. I swear, we'll fix everything up hunky-dory, good as new when we get there. It'll all work out, you'll see.

Chapter Six and a Sixth

out of the barn

*F*irst this: When Zack became un-girlfriended (having been dumped by Bess), do you think Abby's crush was still quietly strong and healthy—ready to take up where it left off back in chapter one and a half? Or (question two) after the squirmy *Cold Shoulder* episode, do you suppose her crush either fainted, sickened, weakened, or slipped into a bit of a coma? Or do you (THREE) believe it croaked altogether, with X's for eyes and its little crush feet in the air?

If you chose THREE—death—then the next question is, Did it come back to life (like some creature in a horror movie)? Or had it been squelched beyond hope of resurrection to the point of being Dead as a Doornail? (Although what exactly makes a doornail deader than other nails, or what's particularly dead about *nails* as opposed to, say, *hammers,* I haven't a clue.)

And how about the fact that Abby knows way more about Zack (now that she's been to all those soccer games and watched Bess slog through endless reams of potty jokes)? Knowing more about a guy usually makes it *much* harder to keep a solid crush on him, in my personal opinion.

When the breakup news came, Abby stood very still and asked herself the above questions (but not necessarily in the above order), including the one about nails. That made her peer down at her fingernails, which were polished in a very easy-to-chip grayish color that everyone hated but her. (Nail-polish chipping was Abby's second-favorite pastime after doodling.) She was in her dad's bedroom, facing his wall of mirrored closet doors.

No, wait, *first* Abby was downstairs hearing the news secondhand. It was Cristy who'd called (not Bess). And finally (as promised in chapter six), here's what was said:

Cristy: "Hey, guess what."

Abby: (unprepared, innocent as a lamb, and swallowing a mouthful of leftover lasagna) "Mmph?"

Cristy: "Bess broke up with Zack."

Abby: "Get out!"

Cristy: "For reals!"

Abby's fast questions: "When? Where was I?"

Cristy's reply: "At school, after you left."

"How come she didn't tell *me* she was gonna?" Abby asked.

"I dunno, but Bess says she's totally relieved. She says Zack was getting to be a total drag."

"Really?"

"Yeah. That's what she says."

"Well, how come she called *you* first?"

"I dunno. Why shouldn't she?"

"I guess."

(Pause while both girls mull that over.)

Then Abby: "Was Zack surprised?"

Cristy: "Bess says it blew him away. She's worried sick about him."

Abby: "Wow!"

(More mulling.)

Cristy: "Yeah, well. See you later." And she was gone.

Abby felt a wave of pure happiness wash over her— mixed with sympathy and concern for Zack, of course. Blew him away? Worried sick about him? Was Zack broken-hearted? Crying? Should she call him? Be sympathetic?

The phone was still in her hand. Abby knew Zack's number down to her chip-nailed fingertips, having called it at least THREE hundred times in the old days (always thoughtfully hanging up before anyone actually answered).

Let's freeze on Abby itching to dial and leave her in her dad's den, while we peek into Cristy's apartment for a second.

See? There she is, also grinning from ear to ear. We can imagine why *Abby* would be happy about this breakup, but why is Cristy smiling like that? Simple. Because she thinks the boyfriend thing is over and done with. Finished at last! Cristy figures Bess tried it and didn't like it, and on top of the better-forgotten-so-forget-it Max mess, and all earlier disasters, she thinks Bess is probably cured for life!

There was no telling Cristy that once this boy-girl stuff begins, it never ends. There's no putting the horse back in the barn, as the old saying goes, although how dumb is that? *Of course* you put the horse back in the barn—every single night! Girls liking boys, however, is nothing at all like horses *in* or *out* of barns.

And here's the first example that comes to mind: Bess's great-grandfather (who has been out of the barn for a long, long time) is now THREE-quarters dotty from "age and hard living." He lives in a rest home, although he rarely rests and we *never* call it that. We call it "an assisted-living residence," because they assist him with practically every single thing he does, since he can no longer remember to close his door, or remember *where* his door *is,* let alone find the key.

But the point is that he *did* find another resident there named Mrs. Wrinkleworth, who also requires a ton of assistance. But whether or not she can tell if her daughter is her daughter or her sister or just some nice lady who brings apples (that are really pears), Mrs. Wrinkleworth likes Bess's great-grandfather, and he likes her, and neither of them is the least bit confused about *that.*

So Cristy has another think coming as far as Bess being finished with boys, and she may as well wipe that silly grin off her face.

Meanwhile, back in the den, Abby (wisely) decided to put down the phone and think things through before calling Zack.

Carrying the sweet breakup news, Abby danced past Spencer and Wheezy (who were respectively fighting with and eating action figures on the stairs), and slipped into her dad's room. She closed his door, thinking, Tra la la la la! I knew it would never last! (which is not strictly true). And, Hee-hee-ho-ho-ha! I totally *knew* Bess could never appreciate Zack the way I do!

Then there she was, smiling back at herself in the mirror. (Isn't it interesting that Bess and Zack's breakup made both Cristy and Abby so smiley?)

Abby and her reflection communicated silently, as if they were psychic. Abby telepathically asked her reflection how she felt (meaning *really* felt) about Zack. And how she (Abby) would feel about having a *used* boyfriend. She figured now that Zack had had *one* girlfriend, it would be like potato chips, one leading unstoppably to the next. In fact, sometimes one chip leads to a whole bag, including those salty bits at the bottom, until the eater's lips hurt and tongue swells. But it has to be a *big* bag to achieve that effect, and Zack had only had one official girlfriend as far as Abby knew, unless he'd had a secret harem on the sly, like at Hebrew school or some other hidden place.

The Abbys pondered this: Now that Zack had tried a starter, rehearsal, warm-up girlfriend (Bess), was he ready for the real thing (Abby)???

But then the Abbys' attention wandered out the window, following their ears, which had detected the tinkling tune of Beethoven's Fifth Symphony, which meant only one thing: The ice cream truck!

Mmmm, the Abbys thought, a Choco-Taco would be perfectly *deeeelish* right now. Way better than chips. Remember back in chapter one and a THIRD when I said that Abby constantly (but unconsciously) had Zack on her mind like background music? I think I compared it to not realizing that you're hearing the neighbors' air conditioner until the noise stops and you go, Ahhh! Silence! Well, the Zack noise stopped right about here (never to return, I'm guessing) and Beethoven took over.

Abby glanced back at her reflection as a strange sensation came over them both. They realized simultaneously that the feeling wasn't just sugar craving. It was sugar craving mixed with *boredom*! Not only did the prospect of Zack not thrill and obsess Abby as it had in the old days, but it even *bored* her!

This crush had absolutely gone back in the barn! The Abbys felt totally *over* it. They turned and soon lost sight of each other in their haste to catch the ice cream man.

Okay, now we can go back to Abby calling Bess about

Emma. I know it got a little twisty, but there are just so many details, details, details, you wouldn't believe. And isn't time travel thrilling?

Note to Mr. Wordsmith: *Yes,* I read your handout on outlining, but not *everyone* can work that way. And wasn't that whole mirror thing artistic? Don't you think the narrator should get extra credit for that?

Chapter Six
and Two THIRDS

a metaphorical (non-violent) call to arms

We're back in Abby's dad's den, which is a fairly amazing coincidence since that's exactly where she was when she got the call from Cristy telling her that Bess had broken up with Zack! And the coincidence is even more astonishing when you consider that Abby has two houses and each one has a whole slew of phones all over the place(s). In fact, the phones are *so* all-over-the-place that often the only way to find them is to listen for the rings.

Abby marched to her dad's desk to try again. (Remember? She was calling Bess to tell her to leave Emma's Zack, meaning *Fred,* alone.) This time Bess answered. The call went like this:

Wait, first I should say that when Abby sat down, she

automatically opened the desk drawer to grab a pen and paper because (as you know) she was a compulsive doodler (as well as a nail-polish chipper), especially when she was on the phone or in class. Some people may think this meant she was creative, but I bet if you actually lived with her, it would be totally annoying to turn your back on a piece of paper for two seconds and have it be so doodled up (and sometimes smeared with lipstick kisses) that you wouldn't even recognize it when you returned. And if you had an important message or phone number or homework assignment written there, tuff.

So Abby opened the drawer to get doodling supplies, and there staring back at her was the name *Zack* written in hundreds of different curly, flowery ways, with hearts. Page after page after page (flip, flip) on the message pad.

She must not've sat at this desk for a while, because she swore she'd gathered up and shredded all these Zacks ages ago. (Except, of course, the ones that were carved in things like pajama drawers.)

Anyway, back to the phone. Ring, ring. "Good evening. Bafoofnick residence, Bess speaking."

"Hello, Bess, this is your friend and classmate Abigail Falzetta. I hope I'm not disturbing you."

"Not at all, Abby! It's always a pleasure to hear from you. How have you been?"

"Quite well. Thank you for asking. And how are you and your family?"

Just kidding. That was to remind you of the earlier bit about everyone's manners being lousy, which was pretty random in the first place, I admit.

Their conversation really went like this:

Abby, in a fairly snotty tone, said, "Ya know, *Bess,* Fred already *has* a girlfriend."

Bess: "Huh?"

Abby: "You heard me."

Bess: "*Sheeesh,* what's *your* problem?"

Abby: "Just think about it!"

Then Abby hung up. And Bess looked at the phone in her hand, rolled her eyes, and said, "What-ever," to herself.

Abby did not feel satisfied. By the time she'd finished her homework, she was convinced that she had to warn Emma! But her homework (thanks to social science) had taken so long that it was way too late to call Emma's house. Plus, Abby was at her dad's and her phone book was at her mom's. She didn't know Emma's number by heart because they weren't *that* good friends. And it was time for bed.

Two hours later when Abby *still* couldn't fall asleep, she flopped onto her back and thought, It's my *responsibility* to stop Bess from doing to Emma what she did to me!

By morning, the Fred-Emma romance (in Abby's sleep-starved mind) was a fragile, timid, endangered thing, as precious and delicate as a newly hatched butterfly, unfurling its new wings on the very edge of extinction.

And Bess had grown so powerful and mighty (in Abby's head) that she was practically a volcanic tornado, meaning an unstoppable destructive force of nature. And boy-girl-wise Abby now thought of Bess as an irresistibly gorgeous supermodel-diva beauty-queen movie star instead of a regular, cute-but-not-all-that-amazing seventh-grade girl. Abby was sure that Emma and Fred couldn't possibly stand a chance against *Super Bess!* In other words, Abby and reality had parted ways.

Never mind how Abby herself had (not that long ago) said that Emma was an annoying little twit and Fred a totally obnoxious geek. By the time Abby rushed out the door on that particular Friday, she thought of Emma and Fred as helpless ants whereas Bess was a monstrous spray can of insecticide. They were innocent lambs to Bess's slaughterhouse. Weeds to her whacker.

In the face of such immediate danger, Abby didn't think there was time to beg Bess to show mercy. No, Abby felt it her *duty,* her *mission,* her *quest* to get to school early and be on the alert for ways to prevent emotional disaster! Abby waited at the door until Emma showed up, then pounced like a tiger. Clutching at Emma's sleeve, Abby hissed, "Bess likes *Fred*!!!"

To which Emma (surprised, needless to say) replied, "So?"

Abby tightened her grip, figuring Emma must not have understood. She spoke more slowly, more carefully. "Bess *likes* Fred. *Your* Fred."

Emma looked from Abby's wild eyes to Abby's white-knuckled grip on her sleeve, and said, "And . . . ?"

Abby blinked a few dozen times, then said, "What do you mean, 'And . . . ?' He's your *boyfriend*!"

Emma shrugged one shoulder and said, "Oh, please."

Chapter Seven

the icky part

But Abby was not discouraged! With much undetected note passing during history and whispering in the hall between classes, Abby managed to communicate to *everyone* that there was something seriously secret, and secretly serious, going on right here, right now.

And to Bess, Abby made it perfectly crystal clear that the secret something did *not* include her. All Bess knew was that her two best friends and her two emergency friends were over there together—without her. On purpose. Every now and then one of them would turn around, *not* to call her over, but to shoot icy-cold smirks at her.

Note: Sticks and stones may break your bones, but mean looks can *really* mess you up.

Often in books and TV shows when your friends suddenly cut you off with no explanation, it means they're planning your surprise birthday party. But Bess's birthday wasn't till August and that was why she suddenly melted into actual *tears* right there on the ramp outside the library bungalow.

Look at her. Isn't it so sad? Tears and snot dripping down her face, and no one to comfort her. I *hate* this part!

If I could, I'd march right up to that nasty little clique of clods and wag my finger and give them a stern lecture on compassion and the true value of friendship. *That* would help, don't you think? Just kidding.

It occurs to me that I told you about Dawn's mom, Fim (and her sister, Biela), and since you know all about Bess's mom, Lindy, and Abby's and Cristy's moms, it seems wrong not to say *something* about Emma's.

I realize this might not be the right time since you're probably dying to find out what's going to happen with Abby and Bess and all that, but if I don't do it *now*, I may never get to it, and then if Emma's mom reads this, she might *pretend* she couldn't care less, but she could be secretly hurt deep inside, and you never know how people will act out later when they've been covering pain. I mean, look at Abby! *She* may think her defense of Emma against Bess has nothing in the world to do with revenge for the Zack thing, but I don't buy that. Do you?

So in the interest of equality I'd just like to say this: Emma's mom was very nice. Okay?

And Emma's family was *nothing* like Fred's, that's for sure. But since Fred's family (according to Mr. Wordsmith) has not one tiny bit of connection to this particular story, forget I even mentioned it or else you'll get caught up in questions like, Why did Fred's mom continue her hopelessly pathetic romance with Dr. Y? Why didn't she see that Dr. Y would never change? Why didn't her friends and relatives set her straight? Why did Fred's mom put her beloved son (Fred) through that? And why didn't she realize what a huge mistake it all was? Why? Why? Why this? Why that? In fact, all those whys are why I named him Dr. Y.

Remember: All names are changed to protect the innocent (and the guilty), and to keep me from getting sued. Oh! Maybe *that's* why Mr. Wordsmith thought I should drop Dr. Y from the story. If anyone is likely to sue me, it would be Dr. Y!

Note: Now that we're on the subject of names (such as Dr. Y), the question is, What shall I name *this* story? Possible title ideas (so far) include: *Those THREE, THREE Best Friends, Wobbly THREES, THREE Girls and a Boy,* and *The THREE Little Pigs,* although that one has been used. But in case I don't actually absolutely *have* to use the word THREE in there, I could call this story *He's Mine!* or *The ABCs.* I had two or THREE other titles that I can't recall right this second, but I'm pretty sure none of them were that great.

Oh yeah, first I thought of *THREE for All*—like free-for-all, get it? And *that* led me to the patriotic ones like *Let THREEDOM Ring* and *My Country 'Tis of THREE,* etc., which I thought were such a crack-up at first that I nearly peed my pants. But I'm past that.

Any ideas? You can think about it (quietly, in the *back* of your mind) and let me know later if you come up with anything.

Chapter Seven and a Half

multi-generational exclusion

Wanna know what happened next? Well, tough. Just kidding, of course, but it *is* pretty much up to *me* what you're going to know and when you're going to know it. In fact, if I weren't so nice, I could give out the story in piddly little bits, teasing you until you want to tear your hair out, or making you flip ahead to the last page or heave the book into the fish tank. But don't. I did that once, and the glue from the binding dissolved and made the water all cloudy and the next day Finlips (my goldfish) was swimming clumsily sideways in a very unfishlike, hard-to-watch way. Then he sort of half-swam/half-floated for two very long, very miserable days, after which I found him crunched up dead under the filter, which was sad but also gross.

So, in order to save *your* goldfish from a similar demise, I'll move this story along by telling you that although Bess is sad and hurt *now,* in a couple more pages she'll actually "*hate* Abby's stinking guts" (her words, not mine). Remember back in chapter THREE when I warned you that THREES in friendships can be wobbly? Well, this is *exactly* the kind of thing I meant! Poor Bess on the outs, trying not to cry but crying anyway, all alone on the playground. Sigh.

But the thing I personally find amazing is how *long* it took for these THREE girls to divide up and turn against one another. I had two friends for a (very) short while in middle school, and we were absolute *cannibals,* skinning each other alive and tearing each other limb from limb. I swear, just remembering how we treated each other gives me hives. But my THREESOME experience is unimportant compared to the fact that *no one* in the whispering circle asked Abby *why* she was suddenly so gung-ho about protecting the Emma-Fred relationship.

It seemed particularly strange and threatening to *Cristy* that Abby was willing to turn against one of her sworn best friends over something as dim and slippery as a single mention of some boy being funny. But Cristy didn't speak up for a whole bunch of reasons, not the least of which was that it had been *she* who told Abby about Bess thinking Fred was funny in the first place (although who'd have guessed it would cause such turmoil and bloodshed?).

Cristy had a hunch that this was just one more bizarre

symptom of the boy-girl disease that everyone else seemed to have caught. She didn't want to let on that the whole thing didn't make a speck of sense to her, because even *hinting* that might make all the other girls turn their sharp-eyed attention on *her*—on her crushless heart, her breast-less chest, her lack of hatred for their teachers, her love of soccer, and all her other weirdnesses and weaknesses. Including her fondness for school cafeteria food (which she dared to eat only on momentous occasions or when Abby and Bess were *both* absent, which was practically never).

Plus, Cristy figured that if Abby could turn so abruptly against Bess, with whom she had boy-craziness in common, then imagine how easily she could dump Cristy!

I'm not sure, but maybe when Bess ran to the bathroom to hide her red face, Cristy ditched the herd, ducked in behind her, and asked, "Bess? You okay?"

I hope she did, because Bess really had absolutely no idea what had hit her, and she sure could've used a friend and a clue. Plus, it would make sense that Cristy would do that, because she probably felt guilty about turning her back on her pal Bess for no good reason. Especially since Cristy thought of herself as *the nice one* of the THREE. Or maybe Cristy cast off her nice-girl sugar coating and entered the bathroom as a spy, consumed by curiosity.

But I have no actual hard evidence that Bess and Cristy met in the john, and I don't want to make stuff up. The only thing I know for a *fact* is that out in that huddle Cristy did *not* defend Bess against Abby.

Oh, and I also know this: When Bess tried to figure out what everyone was so mad at her about, she remembered that she'd called Abby the night before last (to talk about Lindy's roots) and that Abby hadn't seemed to care and had never called back. Aha! Bess thought. That must mean this started as far back as chapter five! Bess wondered what she'd done to make Abby and everyone so mad, but she couldn't think of a single thing.

You and I know why Abby didn't call Bess back: pie. But (oops!) come to think of it, I never did tell you what *Bess* thought at the time.

Well, I probably forgot because it was no big deal. Bess *herself* hadn't given it a single solitary thought until now. So you can pity her all you want about the current situation at school, but I hope you didn't worry about her on account of the unreturned call. If you did, I apologize. I was just so busy telling you about Lindy's chanting, and Abby's mom kissing Steve, and the green pepper incident, that I forgot. Plus, there was that whole thing about fixing the parents up with each other. No wait, that came *before* the bit about Lindy's roots. Now that you mention it, I'm not exactly sure *why* I didn't tell you how Bess felt about Abby not calling her back when she'd said she would. Wait here a second while I go back and check.

Yes! Of course, I had to explain about Cristy being allergic to peanuts (although that doesn't sound as important now as it must have then). And after *that* we got into the whole discussion about breakups in general and Bess and Zack's breakup in particular. And next thing we knew, we were meeting Dawn and her mom, Kim, and Dawn's best friend, Emma, and then Fred . . .

So as you can see, although Bess's life is a mess right *now,* it went on happily enough for pages and pages after not being called back by Abby. Even the very same night as the no-call-back, Bess hadn't spent a single split second drumming her fingers. In fact, it's entirely possible that if Abby *had* called back, she would've gotten the answering machine.

Well, that's a lie. Lindy was all over that phone at any hint of a ring, and she wouldn't have let the machine get anywhere near it. But if Abby had called, then as soon as Lindy realized that she wasn't Er-*ick,* she would've made Abby hang up. Mostly because Lindy couldn't bear the idea of Er-*ick* finally calling only to get discouraged by a busy signal, but also partly because they were in the middle of a film.

You see, Gilda had come home with THREE rented horror movies. Bess and Gilda and their mom had climbed into Lindy's high bed and spent the evening scared stiff, hysterically shoving caramel corn into their faces.

When it came time to go to sleep, all THREE curled up like a litter of mice under Lindy's soft blankie and slept in the crumbs, while a few blocks away Abby's brother, Spencer, began barfing his brains out. But that's ancient history. The bathroom doesn't even smell anymore, so there you go. (Is it my imagination or is there a lot of vomit in this story?)

But more important for now: Back in the "lunchroom," there was Emma, giddy over Abby's sudden attention, because Abby was considered by some people (including Emma) to be fairly popular. Meanwhile, Abby didn't know it yet, but the idea of losing Fred was way, way less upsetting to Emma than Abby had thought. And that's because Emma was beyond sick to death of Fred, and she'd been trying to dump him forever.

The reason Emma'd had no luck shaking Fred was because he was too dense to get it that she couldn't stand him. She'd considered saying, "You make me sick, you stupid little creep!" But that didn't seem nice. And anyway, having a boy madly in love with you was kind of flattering and it impressed people, even if the boy was only Fred.

Nonetheless, Emma was tempted at first to tell Abby to warn Bess that Fred was a royal pain in the butt as a boyfriend. But she decided to keep her mouth shut. She figured Bess would find out soon enough when Fred started calling Bess's house constantly (instead of Emma's) and hanging up (bang!) if anyone but Bess answered.

Emma snickered (on the inside), imagining how peaceful life would be without Fred's THREE zillion daily calls (just to say hi). The most recent call (and several dozen before that) went like this:

Emma: (answering the phone) "Hello?"

Fred: "Hi."

Emma: "Oh, it's you."

Fred: "I just wanted to say hi."

Emma: "Humph."

Fred: "Well, talk to you later."

Emma: "No, don't call la—"

Phone: Click!

Emma's whole family would cheer if Fred switched his attention to Bess! Especially Emma's big brother, Luke, who had threatened (or should I say *offered*) to reach down Fred's throat and pull out his beating heart with his bare hands (which was sweet). But now Emma realized that thanks to Bess, Luke might not have to spend the rest of his life in prison for murder. Hooray!

But you're probably more curious about what was being whispered in the girl huddle near the drinking fountain, so here goes:

Abby: "I love Bess like a sister, but I just can't let her do this to you!"

Emma: (mumbling) "Oh, that's okay."

Abby: "No. It's. Not. It's *not* okay for her to cause you pain!"

Emma: "Well." (shrug)

Dawn: "Gee!" (I told you she had a small part but that's no reason to leave her out entirely.)

And Bess (all alone, way over there): Sniffle.

Was Abby such a meanie that she *liked* making one of her best friends suffer? Heavens, no. She was enormously sorry to hurt Bess, but she felt it simply *had* to be done. No choice here.

And what was Abby getting out of all this? The knowledge that she was a better person than everyone else. Example: Had *anyone* taken the trouble to stick up for Abby's right to eternal dibs on Zack? The answer was no. Would Abby let the little snag that Emma didn't particularly *want* her romance with Fred defended, stop her from doing what she knew was right? No again. So there you go.

Elsewhere (on the subject of leaving out and excluding), Lindy's boyfriend Er-*ick* was planning to go to his big rowdy family reunion picnic without Lindy. If he'd snuck off and reunited without telling Lindy about it in the first place, then so what? But just last week he'd gone on and on about how she'd *love* his nephew Dipstick and his niece Bilebreath and he even told Lindy she'd have to yell when she spoke to his deaf (gruff on the outside, gruff on the inside) uncle Belch. And wait till she tasted his mom's puke soup! (See? Vomit again.)

And Lindy had said, "Yummm!"

Lindy had torn through her closets, holding up each article of clothing for Bess to grade. In the A pile went innocent country-girl picnic clothes. In the B pile went slightly sexy city-girl picnic clothes. All the rest were dumped on the chair. Lindy and Bess had also discussed possible hairstyles for the all-important meeting of Er-*ick*'s family.

Gilda (who dressed like a cross between a truck driver and a soldier, but in a tasteful and interesting way) did not allow herself to be drawn into the degrading grading of clothing. Nor did she sink to taking an active part in the seemingly endless discussion of whether to braid or not to braid, ponytail or bun? In fact, Gilda did little more than roll her eyes at Lindy's costuming concerns.

But if Gilda had been absolutely *forced* to cast a vote, she probably would've voted for the jean skirt and red T-shirt, with hair in a loose orange ponytail (because Gilda secretly liked the cowgirl look, when it wasn't too overdone or corny).

But it doesn't matter, because after all of that, Er-*ick* mumbled something yesterday about families being such a (this is a quote) "snake pit of old grievances" that he felt he and Lindy should (further quote) "keep their relationship free of family stress," yadda, yadda. And that he and Lindy should (this is the clincher) "strive to maintain their individuality and privacy." Plus, he said, "You'd just be bored." Which meant only one thing to Lindy, and that was that Er-*ick* didn't care enough about her to introduce her to his folks.

Ouch. That hurt.

If you're thinking maybe Er-*ick*'s change of heart about taking Lindy to his family reunion didn't mean anything, you're wrong. And if you think he just chickened out *this time* but would soon proudly introduce Lindy to his relatives, you're wrong again. And if you're thinking that he is going to call any minute now, or even any *day* now, with a fabulous explanation and lots of love, you're *still* wrong. And if you insist on continuing along this wrongful path, it will no doubt end badly for you. And here's why:

Because even if you're not an all-out bimbo, you're probably a *misguided optimist*—like Lindy. Meaning you trust everyone too much and think we're all going to live happily ever after in a land of smiling flowers and sunny skies where everyone is honest and brave and kind and cheerful and no innocent people get sick and die in agony.

The point is, forget Er-*ick*. He's scum. My fondest dream is to see Er-*ick* and (boo-hiss) Jonas adrift together mid-ocean aboard a paddle-less, sunblock-less raft without life jackets. And what's this? High seas? A darkening sky? A wicked typhoon brewing? Ha!

BONUS:

Here are the answers to some other questions you may have.

Q) Does Lindy have any clue *why* Er-*ick* suddenly uninvited her to the picnic?

A) None.

Q) Does Abby feel guilty about making her best friend cry?

A) Not yet, but she will in chapter eight.

Q) Are we ever going to hear what happened between Bess and Max?

A) No. So forget it.

Chapter Eight

bad feelings all around

Remember when I'd said that Cristy only allowed herself to eat school cafeteria food on momentous occasions or when Abby and Bess were both absent? Well, for Cristy, the upside of these troubling times was that the troubles were momentous enough to allow her to buy lunch! So at exactly noon, Cristy was standing at the end of the lunch line, wondering where she should sit. Over there, Abby was with Emma and Dawn. And all the way over *there* where the wall *would* be if this were a real room, Bess sat alone with her eyes spronged out like she'd been clonked on the head. Cristy tipped her tray one way, then the other, making her carton of milk slide back and forth.

Meanwhile Abby was *not* enjoying Emma's tuna breath, nor Emma's lack of gratitude for her (Abby's) self-sacrificing interest in saving her (Emma's) romance! Plus, in her (Abby's) haste to get to school to warn Emma about Bess, Abby had forgotten to pack a lunch, and now she was starving and neither Emma nor Dawn was offering her the least crumb.

After all that Abby had done for her, shouldn't Emma . . . Well, out of gratitude, at least, don't you think Emma should . . .

Note: *Shoulds* are always a problem when it comes to human behavior. Yes, maybe Emma *should* have read Abby's mind, or read her stomach growls at least, and realized Abby was hungry. And yes, I suppose it would've been nice if Emma had been sensitive enough to know that most people, like herself, got hungry around lunchtime.

Emma *could have* said, "Where's your lunch?" And she *should have* said, "Want to share mine?" I would've done so in the same situation and I'm sure you would too. But Abby could just as well have spoken up and said, "I forgot my lunch. Can you spare a crust of bread?" Right?

Could have, should have . . . the fact remains that Emma ate, Abby didn't. And actually, if Abby had looked closer at the tuna salad churning in Emma's half-open mouth, she'd have seen tiny flecks of green. And those flecks were not sweet-pickle relish, nor were they parsley or celery. They were green bell pepper!

So if Emma *had* offered some to Abby and Abby had accepted, she would've been sorry later. And her day was already going to be quite bad enough without adding relentless green burps, as you will soon see.

Which reminds me, as it probably reminds you, of that picnic on the beach with Steve when he remembered not to put bell peppers in the potato salad. There are two different picnics in this story, but we do *not* care about the one with Er-*ick*. In fact, we hope there's a terrible electrical storm flash flood with hail and the Er-*ick* reunion picnic is canceled or worse.

We couldn't confuse the two picnics anyway, because one was nothing but a source of pain to Lindy, who had never harmed a fly and did *not* deserve to be rejected or uninvited, having been hurt plenty in the past already. Whereas the other picnic was so sweet and lovey it was practically one of those tear-jerking commercials that (after you've gotten all choked up) makes you want to punch someone's lights out for messing with your emotions like that, and all for the lowly, crass, commercial purpose of selling phone services or greeting cards, for Pete's sake.

Nonetheless, I'm going to tell you the missing part of that Steve picnic right now. Ready? It's the part I meant to confess in chapter five (having left it out on purpose before) but forgot to. Remember?

Well, after everyone ate the pepper-free potato salad, the kids chased napkins and seagulls while their mom and Steve smooched. Then Abby, Spencer, and Wheezy returned to the picnic blanket. And that's when, without a moment's hesitation, Spencer climbed right into Steve's great big lap. He just crawled on up there and sat down like a prince on a throne.

Steve didn't act a bit surprised, but Abby couldn't believe it. Must be nice, she thought, to be six and able to do stuff like that. She could tell that Steve's huge body protected Spence from the stinging wind. Then Steve raised his bear-paw-size hand and ever so gently flicked a feather out of Spencer's hair.

That's all. That's what I was keeping from you before. Maybe it's not such a big deal, but at the time it seemed like the last-straw-type thing that would break the camel's back, sweetness-wise.

And it seemed particularly unfair to go on about how great Steve was, the gentle giant and all that, right when Lindy was having such a hard time with Er-*ick*. And speaking of unfairness, it now seems cruelly out of balance that both Bess and her mom should be feeling rejection from two different sources on the same day. But there you go.

Now you know everything I know. So, back to the "lunchroom," where, after a while Abby looked around and saw Cristy (with a full tray of food) just standing there practically hypnotizing herself with her side-to-side milk.

Abby looked in the other direction and spied Bess sitting *way* over there, not eating her peanut butter, banana, and raspberry jam sandwich. Abby could practically *feel* the peanut butter melting on her tongue.

(In case you're worried, it's Cristy, not Abby or Bess,

who's allergic to nuts, as in pea*nut* butter. See how easy it is to forget these things?)

Abby looked from the untouched sandwich to Bess's face, and saw that Bess's eyes were red and swollen. Poor Bess!

Then, ish! Abby got pinged in the forehead by one of Fred's spitballs that had been intended for Emma. Fred wasn't a very good aim, but his heart was true and he was dedicated. Emma had been batting away his spitballs not just since she sat down to eat lunch that day, but at *every* lunch hour since school began in September!

Even Abby, who wasn't all that perceptive, noticed before lunch was over that it was *not* fondness for Fred that she saw in Emma's eyes as Emma chewed and chewed her tuna sandwich with her mouth wide open. Abby couldn't help but watch the tuna and mayo and bread (and green pepper flecks) churning around in there like laundry in the washing machine, but grosser.

So why is Fred her *boyfriend* if she doesn't *like* him? Abby asked herself.

And suddenly Abby *hated* Emma. And she glared at her, thinking, This is all Emma's fault in the first place! Okay, Abby thought next, maybe it's not Emma's *fault*-fault, but it's not like she's totally *blameless*! Then, all the anger gave itself up in one big, deflating sigh. And *that's* when Abby asked herself the classic question: *What have I done???*

Note: Would *that* be a good title? *What Have I Done?* (Think about it.)

Meanwhile, across the room, Bess's mood had also taken a sudden turn—from sad-hurt confusion to mad-furious anger. *How dare they shut me out like this???* She knew that Abby was the brains (if you can call them that) behind this operation, because Cristy (no offense) wasn't the type.

This is where Bess glared in Abby's direction and muttered, "I hate her stinking guts!" under her breath.

And at exactly that second, Emma jutted her chin out at Fred and yelled, "You're such a pathetic loser, Fred! Why don't you go bother Bess? *She's* the one that likes you, not me!"

When Nick, who was sitting next to Fred, heard what Emma said, he jumped to his feet and in less than THREE seconds had catapulted himself across the "lunchroom," past Cristy (who still stood mesmerized by her milk), and landed, grinning his head off, in front of Bess, who was definitely *not* grinning.

Many, many eyes watched Nick, and many ears heard him say, "Wow, Bess, you like *Fred* now?"

Bess's first reaction was to think, *Fred?* Spitball Fred? Pretend-to-trip-and-go-sprawling Fred?

Note: She didn't remember *saying* or even *thinking* anything about Fred recently, and it's a good thing, because if she *had* remembered telling Cristy that she thought Fred was funny, she'd have a great excuse for being even *madder* at everyone, and she was already *plenty* angry enough.

Instead of slugging Nick, though, Bess kept her temper

in check and just gave him the withering look he deserved. "Yeah, right," she said. "Like I'm almost sure." Meaning, *Eeew*.

Then she got up and slammed her uneaten PBB&J into the trash, and stomped out of there. "Harrumph!"

From across the room Abby sprang to her feet and hurried over to Bess to say . . . Well, I don't know *what* she meant to say, because she didn't get a chance to say it! And here's why: When Bess saw her friend (Abby) barreling toward her, she did *not* smile welcomingly with relief. Instead Bess turned sharply and marched away—shoulders back, chin definitely *up*!

Abby (not yet discouraged) followed Bess out of the "lunchroom," yelling, "Hey, Bess! Wait! I need to talk to you!"

But without even turning around, Bess barked, "Tough. I don't want to hear it," and kept marching.

Abby chased Bess a little farther, calling, "But Bess, I'm *sorry*!"

To which Bess answered (over her shoulder), "That's *your* problem."

Abby's voice got shrill. "Come on, Bess! Wait up!" But it didn't do a bit of good. Bess didn't even slow down.

Back in class after the lunchless lunch, Abby felt really terrible. The kind of terrible that's full of guilt and regret and feels a lot like food poisoning mixed with the gut-sinking sensation of a plummeting elevator—on an empty stomach, no less. This was the time when Abby told herself stuff like, "I betrayed my friend!" And, "I'm dirt times THREE!"

At the end of school she tried *again* to get Bess to talk to her, but Bess absolutely *refused* (with a quick turn of the head), leaving Abby standing there all dangling arms and legs, tongue practically lolling out, feeling . . . well, you can imagine how she felt.

And even worse, because not only was one of her best friends not talking to her so badly that she wouldn't even *hear* an apology, but her other best friend had also mysteriously disappeared and wasn't there to say, "Don't worry, Abby, it'll all work out in the end."

Was Cristy still in the "lunchroom" rocking her tray and mesmerizing herself with her milk carton? Oh, who cares where she was. The point (for Abby) was that she had to drag her thoroughly depressed and self-loathing self all the way home alone. Isn't that a sad way to end the chapter?

Chapter Nine

phone frenzy

After Abby threw herself down, sighing dramatically, on just about every piece of furniture in her dad's house, she called Cristy. "I don't know why Bess hates me!" Abby whined.

"Maybe it's 'cause you tried to turn everyone against her," Cristy suggested.

"Yeah, but I thought she was going to go after Fred!"

"I don't really get it," Cristy said.

"Well," said Abby, "remember the Zack thing?"

"What's *Zack* got to do with it?"

"You know."

"No, I don't."

"Well, you should," Abby huffed.

Cristy didn't say anything.

"And I *tried* to apologize after lunch, you know. I *said* I was sorry! But Bess just blew me off! Why do you think she's so mad?"

"I dunno," said Cristy.

"Have you talked to her?" Abby asked.

"I gotta go do my homework," Cristy answered.

"Wait! What did Bess tell you?"

"I dunno," Cristy said, sounding squirmy. "I gotta hang up now, 'kay?" And click, Cristy was gone.

Abby held on to the phone. She could almost swear it was breathing. Then she hung up and paced, ate a few apricots, called her dad at work to see what time he was coming home, squeezed Wheezy, made Spencer turn down the volume on his obnoxious computer game, and looked at herself in the mirror.

While Abby stands there in the bathroom examining her zits, we're going to career over to Cristy's apartment for just a second. It worked pretty well when we did it before, remember? When we caught Cristy grinning about Bess and Zack's breakup? That was the horse-went-back-in-the-barn part. *Now* do you remember? We can't really go on until you are positively positive that you recall the scene, so think about it for a second.

Ready or not, back we go to Cristy's. But I don't want to give anything away plot-wise here, so *don't* look around the room. In fact, just close your eyes while I tell you this one thing that's going on inside Cristy's head: Aha!

"Aha!" might not sound like much to you, but this particular "Aha!" means that Cristy suddenly sees the connection between Bess going for Zack and Abby thinking Bess was going for Fred. Not that it *changes* anything, and not that it's gigantically earth-shattering, but it's better than nothing.

Okay, now (whoosh!) back to Abby. She's done looking in the mirror. Now she's pacing. Now she's picking up the phone and dialing Cristy's number again.

Now speaking: "Hi. It's me. Have you talked to Bess?"

"I'm doing my homework, Abby," Cristy lied. (She hadn't even taken her junk out of her backpack yet.)

"Well, if you talk to her, tell her I'm sorry, 'kay?"

"Okay."

The next time Abby called, the conversation went like this:

Abby: "You talk to Bess yet?"

Cristy: "Jeez, Abby."

Abby: "Jeez what?"

Cristy: "I dunno, just, *jeez*! Couldn't you leave me outta this? I don't wanna be in the middle and I don't even get it, really. But anyway, my mom's gotta use the phone, so, bye."

Then Abby's dad came home and brought tacos. Abby tried to tell him the whole story, but he got everyone's names confused, and at the end all he said was, "Does that mean you'll finally stop writing *Zack* all over everything?"

Gee, thanks, Dad.

Then Abby and Spencer were ponged over to their mom's house. Usually that sort of swift scene change would make a person such as Abby forget what she was obsessing about and move her on to something else. But not this time. Abby considered talking to her mom about the whole mess, but she'd have to start way, way back at the beginning, and what would we do meanwhile? Look how long it's taken us to get this far! Plus, Abby felt much too antsy to stop here for a bunch of useless Q and A with Mom, and I don't blame her.

While Abby's mom and Spencer took Wheezy out back, Abby slipped into the kitchen and, getting a sudden burst of courage, decided to forget Cristy and call Bess herself. She took a deep breath. Ring, ring, ring.

Bess's sister, Gilda, said, "Hello."

"Can I talk to Bess?" Abby asked—quietly, so her mom and Spencer wouldn't hear her, although there'd be nothing odd or suspicious about Abby calling and asking for Bess, as far as Abby's mother or brother (or dog) knew or cared.

Gilda, being the perceptive type, instantly detected something fishy in Abby's tone, and this entire story, *Prologue* through *Epilogue* (everything but the title!), sprang up practically word for word in her head!

Gilda knew all about cliques and girl groups and out-casting. But no matter how clear-sighted a person may be, there is often nothing she can do to alter the course of history other than state the truth and stand back. So, in answer to Abby's heart-wrenching question, "Can I talk to Bess?" Gilda had no choice but to answer, "She's at Cristy's." (See? That's why I didn't want you looking around the room where Cristy had her "Aha!" because right next to Cristy you'd have seen Bess standing there, with a fat orange tabby cat weaving around and through her legs.)

Abby didn't shriek "*Cristy's? She's* been at Cristy's *all this time*???" She didn't drop the phone. She very quietly said, "Oh. Okay, thanks." Then, while Gilda stood there, feeling terrible for the poor kid at the other end of the line, Abby hung up, ran to her room, and pulled the covers over her head.

Once she'd done that, however, Abby just found herself under the blanket with not much air to breathe, and all her problems down under there with her. And talk about breathing, Abby realized with a sick feeling in her gut that the breathing phone she'd heard earlier must've been Bess listening in on Cristy's call. Eeeew!

After the worst of the flinches and winces had passed, Abby crept out and dialed Cristy's. But before I tell you how that call went, I think it's only fair that you know how Bess happened to end up at Cristy's house that day after school. You may think it's not fair for *you* to find out before poor Abby does, but I'm the narrator and I can do whatever I want.

Here are your choices: 1) When Cristy snapped out of her milk-carton trance of indecision, she dumped her tray (so much for her momentous cafeteria-food occasion) and took off after Abby, who was chasing Bess. But (unlike Abby) Cristy stayed on Bess's trail until she caught her and said, "I'm so sorry I ignored you. It was temporary insanity. Plus, it was all Abby's fault. Do you forgive me?"

And Bess said (pant-pant, out of breath from running), "Sure."

2) Cristy was minding her own business in the crowded hall between classes when Bess ran up and practically tackled her! Then Bess fell to her scabby knees in front of absolutely *everyone* and, clutching on to Cristy's clothes, she begged for Cristy to be her friend again. "Oh please!" Bess pleaded. "Please, please, please, please, please?"

And Cristy (blushing wildly, with sweat sponging out of every pore) said, "Jeez, Bess!"

"Pretty please?" Bess groveled, lowering her chin to the floor but keeping her death grip on Cristy's pant leg. Until Cristy, so embarrassed it was making her dizzy, growled, "Okay, okay. Just get up and *cut that out*!!!"

Or 3) (THREE) Bess trapped Cristy alone in the bathroom and (in a scary, hostile tone) threatened, "Cristy, if you don't let me come to your house after school today,

I'm telling your mom about the five-dollar bill you pinched from her jewelry box last year!"

And Cristy gasped, "You wouldn't!"

"Would too!" Bess insisted.

"Would not!" etc., until Cristy said, "Oh, all right then. You can come over."

Ha! Fooled you! It was none of those THREE!

The *real* story is that Cristy thought Bess was in the *right* and Abby was in the *wrong*. So without a thought for her own social security—without a moment's consideration of the very real possibility of contaminating herself by association with the ousted Bess and being ridiculed and excluded by Abby, Emma, and the rest of the girls forevermore, Cristy simply (and bravely) did the right thing and took Bess's side.

Ha-ha-ha-ha! That was a good one! (Sorry, I couldn't resist.)

But now *seriously*, for reals, all jokes aside, here's what truly happened: Bess's mom (Lindy) was so sad about being uninvited to Er-*ick's* family reunion picnic (scheduled for the next day) that she couldn't drag her sorry self out of bed and into the car. All she could manage was to call Cristy's mom and (in a weak and pitiful voice) ask her to please pick up Bess when she fetched Cristy from school. In other words, the girls had nothing to do with this plan and that's the truth.

Yes! Isn't that the perfect title? *The Truth!* It sounds so important and trustworthy! Or maybe *The Whole Truth and Nothing but the Truth So Help Me God*. Well, maybe that's a bit longish, but I think we're on the right track here, don't you?

Anyway, now it was several hours later, and Abby had just found out that Bess had been at Cristy's *all this time*. It absolutely amazed her that Cristy could be so devious and sneaky. Bess maybe, but *Cristy*? Never! Abby cringed, picturing the two of them sitting all cozy together on thrones of books, snickering over Abby's pathetic phone calls while purring cats napped in their laps.

Abby punched out Cristy's phone number so hard she practically broke the phone. When Cristy answered, Abby put on a stony voice and demanded to talk to Bess.

But Cristy didn't gasp at being caught. She just said, "She doesn't want to talk to you right now," and hung up!

Abby looked into the mirror to see if it was really *her* Cristy had spoken to so meanly, and that's when she saw that her bangs needed *emergency* cutting! *Now!* In fact, she couldn't believe she'd actually been walking around in public with them looking like that! Never in the history of hair had a haircut been more urgently needed.

Luckily, the scissors were nearby. Unluckily, they were so dull that they hacked more than they snipped. First it was good on this side but too short on the other, then oops! the sides switched! Abby chopped and sawed until: Phew! What a relief! The offensive bangs were gone. Way gone. (All over the sink and the bathroom rug.)

Abby did not have any fun that evening. And all night long she stumbled between these THREE thoughts:

1) They're so mean! Tricking me! Sneaking behind my back! Making me chop off my hair! Now I have to wear hats and it's all their fault!

2) I hate them.

And 3) (THREE) They hate *me* and I deserve it.

It seemed like morning would never come.

Chapter Ten

a lousy weekend

Morning came, but it didn't do much good because it was Saturday. And it was a Mom Saturday, meaning Abby had to spend the morning sailing. Their first port was perfect for Abby's mood: gloomy. It was an estate sale at a dumpy house with stained wallpaper. They were selling an adult potty seat and walker, and grim-looking medical things mixed in with pictures of clowns on grubby plates and in beat-up-looking frames. The whole place smelled.

Abby wandered around until she got creeped out by the forks with so much crud dried between the tines that they were practically spoons. She ended up standing with her hat pulled low and her hands in her pockets. Spencer waited by the door, holding his nose, while their mom bought a dusty set of pudding cups out of pity. (It turned out that THREE were chipped.)

Then it started to drizzle, then pour. So they cut their sail short and went straight to Flip's Flapjacks, where they were handed menus by a total stranger!

"Where's Nancy?" Spencer asked, glaring at the new waitress as if she'd murdered Nancy and hidden the body herself.

"Can I start y'all with something to drink?" the stranger asked, cracking her gum and ignoring Spencer's question.

They ordered their usual breakfast, but it didn't taste the same.

The day crept by, inch by miserable inch. Even Mr. Rose, Abby's cello teacher, who was usually good for a few laughs, in a musical sort of way, was much less fun than usual, since it was obvious that Abby hadn't practiced all week.

Back home, whenever the phone rang, Abby answered in an extra-cheerful voice in case it was Bess or Cristy, so they'd know she was having a great time without them. But it was never them. When her mom's friends called, they all responded to Abby's perky "Hello!" as if they were talking to the happiest kid on earth. But it was incredibly hard (in fact, it was impossible) for Abby to keep up that chipper tone throughout an entire conversation, so each caller hung up feeling like she had *personally* disappointed or offended Abby somehow.

That night Steve came over with an edible checker set, so apparently he was not consumed with paralyzing guilt over practically killing Abby's little baby brother with pie. In fact edible checkers sounded to Abby like yet *another* attempt on their lives. She squinted up at him, to show that she was onto his tricks, but she had to tip her head so far back that her cap fell off.

Steve squinted back down at her and said, "Neat haircut!"

Abby didn't know if he was teasing or what. She jammed her cap back down over her stubble, as Steve went on to say, "I wish I had the courage to shave my head, but you've got to be smooth to be cool. My brothers clobbered me so many times, I'm all lumpy-headed." He pointed over his left temple. "Eighteen stitches here." He turned to point to the back of his head. "Nine here. Don't recall how many here . . ."

"My hair's not shaved," Abby said, annoyed. "I got it caught in a door." As soon as she said that, she realized how dumb it sounded, but there you go. It was said and she'd have to stand by it.

All Steve said was, "Ow! Bet *that* hurt!" Then he challenged her to a checker game, but Abby said she didn't want to play. Steve offered her first choice of the raspberry or chocolate team, but she said, "No thanks," and Steve didn't beg.

No one had to *beg* Spencer, that's for sure. He had no pride whatsoever and was all over that game. He gobbled up each piece he jumped, and cracked up left and right. Steve was Mr. Jolly Ho-Ho-Ho tonight too, and Abby's mother was doing more than her share of laughing, considering there's nothing all *that* hilarious about checkers.

In any case, Abby thought their laughter made an ironic sound track for her own humorless life.

Plus, unless Steve was the worst checker player in the history of the world, Abby could tell he was letting Spencer win *on purpose,* which irritated Abby no end, so she mostly stayed in her room (not that anyone noticed).

On Sunday morning, Abby called Bess's house, but Gilda (sounding sorry) said Bess was still asleep. And Sunday afternoon, Lindy (sounding stuffy-nosed) told Abby that Bess was taking a nap. Abby had never before known Bess to be such a *sleepy* person.

Chapter Ten and a Half

the Cristy mystery
(isn't that a cute chapter heading?)

*H*ere's a chapter for Mr. Wordsmith and the rest of you who wonder what Cristy was up to during all this. And although I wish I had THREE choices to give you, there are only two, unless you think it's possible that Cristy was thinking, Oh, good! Abby and Bess are finally fighting! I've always hoped they'd have it out!!!

Maybe you figure that as long as Cristy was safely ringside (so she wouldn't catch a stray punch or get spattered with gore), she'd enjoy a fight the way she loved a good soccer match. That's the spectator gene she got from her (football-addicted) dad's side of the family. And it's true that no one has control over the characteristics they inherit genetically. But even though Cristy took Bess home with her after school and allowed Bess to eavesdrop on

Abby's phone call(s), I seriously doubt (in spite of appearances and evidence to the contrary) that Cristy *chose* to take sides and root *for* Bess *against* Abby.

So forget it. I'm not offering that as one of the possibilities. Well . . . okay, I guess I'm offering it as Choice Number One. But take it from me: Choices number two and even THREE are both *much* more likely to be correct.

Here's Choice Number Two: Cristy thought of herself as the peacemaker, the one most likely to grow up to be a self-sacrificing do-gooder type. (After having at least a *little* fun first, which is totally normal. Lots of famous martyr types had a little fun before cheerfully taking on lives of pure hardship, right?)

So Cristy (our hero) thought she was helping *both* sides mediate this dispute. She saw herself as an example of fair open-mindedness and she took it upon herself to work toward a peaceful resolution of this conflict to discover a healthy middle ground where Abby and Bess could co-exist in joyful harmony. What a gal!

Choice Number THREE: Cristy wished her friends would settle this mess themselves and leave her O-U-T of it! Possible quote: "Wake me when it's over. It's not like I don't have enough problems of my own, you know!"

You pick.

Although I'd pick number two. Wanna know why? Because last summer, Cristy (in a bold, uncharacteristic stroke of independence) volunteered part-time at a park, helping with mentally challenged children. And she hardly flinched even when they pulled her hair with their little snot-crusty hands. She'd tried to get Abby and Bess to volunteer there too, but ha! One six-second visit to the park put the kibosh on *that* idea.

The whole scene had freaked Abby out so badly that she wore her bike helmet everywhere, including the bathtub, for the next THREE days (because most of the kids were brain-scrambled from freakish head injuries). Abby admired Cristy for being able to work there, and she told herself that, on the bright side, if she ever got her marbles permanently rattled, at least Cristy would be a pro at helping out. Abby had bad dreams not only of getting her own skull bashed in, but also of being forced to work there alongside Cristy. Abby didn't know which of the nightmares was more nightmarish, as both made her wake up screaming.

Bess, on the other hand, wasn't frightened by the kids Cristy cared for. And unlike Abby, Bess figured that nothing like *that* could ever happen to *her*. What Bess couldn't get a handle on was why anyone would volunteer for *anything*. She couldn't for the life of her get why someone who didn't absolutely *have* to would spend summer mornings being "helpful."

"You're not even getting paid!" Bess said, shaking her head in amazement at Cristy. "You must be as screwy as *they* are!"

Chapter Eleven

time

Bess's sister, Gilda, who'd had her driver's license for less than two months, and who'd spent almost every moment of those two months begging for the car keys, said she'd drop Bess off at school on Monday, saving Lindy the trip. Actually, Gilda's offering to drive Bess wasn't entirely about wanting to drive. It was also about helping poor Lindy, who was such a total wreck that it was scary.

And Lindy said okay because she was so blue over Er-*ick* that she couldn't see straight. But if Lindy thought she was depressed *then*, it was *nothing* compared to the bottomless black pit of agonized self-loathing grief and sorrow to come. Poor Lindy would spend the rest of her miserable life wishing she had never agreed to let Gilda drive. She would regret handing over those car keys with every pitiful breath she took—because the girls were involved in a hideous accident no more than THREE blocks from home.

At this point, I don't think it really truly matters whose fault the accident was. Let it suffice to say that everyone who survived was very, very, very sorry about the tragic loss of such young life. Especially Gilda's life, because she'd shown such promise as a writer and now all her great works would go unwritten. I'm practically in tears writing this, I swear!

And imagine Abby's regret that she'd *never* be able to make up with Bess (and the relentlessly nagging suspicion that *somehow,* if Abby hadn't been such a jerk, Bess would be alive today).

And talk about crying: Cristy was such a mess, it wasn't even funny!

No, that's a terrible way to end a story. Plus, it's mean. And seeing as kids are tragically killed in car accidents left and right, it's in seriously bad taste to joke about it. Not that I was "joking" exactly. I mean, it's not like I expected you to split a gut laughing, for Pete's sake. (And who the heck is *Pete,* anyway?)

But infinitely more important than it not being funny is the fact that in this particular instance it wasn't *true.* Gilda was an exemplary driver and there was no car accident.

I bet you're thinking, Sheesh! If you can't trust a *narrator* to tell the truth, who *can* you trust? And I'm sure there is a valuable lesson there, but we can't stop to discuss it right now because we must hurry on to what really *did* happen.

This: Bess woke up Sunday to the sound of sobbing. She instantly recognized the sobs as Lindy's. And for those first groggy minutes it was like Bess had gone back in time to the boo-hoos over (boo-hiss) Jonas.

You're probably wondering how Bess, still half asleep, could tell what kind of sobbing she was hearing through the wall. How did she know her mom wasn't crying over spilled milk, for instance? Or maybe Lindy had stubbed her toe or cut herself shaving. Or maybe someone had died in some way that had nothing to do with teen drivers.

Well, it's not that Bess was psychic or even particularly sensitive. It's that there had been glaring warning signs (starting with Lindy's roots) that this cry was on its way.

The signs were these:

1) Friday, for the first time in recorded history, Lindy drove Bess to school wearing her bathrobe and *no makeup*. And she was too depressed to pick Bess up after school. (Remember? That's why Bess went home with Cristy?)

2) Saturday (the day of Er-*ick*'s family reunion picnic, which was scheduled from noon to three o'clock) Lindy shlumped around the house all day and checked the phone constantly to make sure it was working. In other words, she was waiting for a call that did not come.

And 3) (THREE) Saturday night Lindy (still in her jammies, and clutching and testing her cell phone) drove to the *Cold Shoulder* and made Bess run in and buy a gallon of mint chocolate chip ice cream and a gallon of cookie dough crunch for Lindy to take home to bed with a spoon.

The first two-part sign (bathrobe in public and no makeup) could've possibly meant Lindy had the flu, but the second (phone checking) and the THIRD (ice cream gorging) were undeniable signs of a breakup.

Poor Lindy.

And poor Bess. It's very hard for a girl to listen to her mom weeping brokenheartedly, even if that girl happens to be thrilled that she won't have to endure any more chanting and that everyone can go back to wearing shoes in the house.

Bess couldn't commiserate with her sister, Gilda, because Gilda was at work, stuffing envelopes for a mail-order place, which was a horrible job with wretched hours that paid lousy and gave Gilda so many paper cuts that her fingers hung in shreds (because being sixteen in the workforce of the real world meant having no rights and being treated like dirt). Plus, Gilda's boss made about THIRTY comments a day about how if Gilda dressed better, she might be pretty. As if she'd want to be *pretty*, and especially as if she'd want to be pretty for some old turd like him. Ick! Ick! Ick! (TRIPLE ick!)

The only thing that kept Gilda going was the thought that one day she could use it all in a novel. And maybe the turd would read it and feel so guilty that after rewriting his will leaving every dime to Gilda as an apology, he'd get hit by lightning. Zap! Twice!

But meanwhile, the turd was alive and well and Gilda was at work, so poor Bess didn't even have her sister to talk to. Not that talking to Gilda would *necessarily* have helped, because although Gilda was a kind and nurturing person by nature, she wouldn't have been terribly sympathetic about this. In fact, I'm fairly sure she would've said something sarcastic like, "You mean Er-*ick* wasn't Prince Charming?" or, "How many frogs is Lindy gonna kiss before she gets it right?"

Part of that was just Gilda's style, making light of bad stuff to cheer up her baby sister. She'd been doing that since forever—about the dark, about spiders, about what it'll be like when their mom dies, about what it will be like when *they* die, etc. And the other part was this: The (boo-hiss) Jonas disaster had been Gilda's last straw, Lindy's-boyfriends-wise. Meaning, it was going to take her a good long time to trust any of Lindy's *true loves* again, if ever.

Anyway, since Gilda wasn't around, Bess wished she could at least call Abby to talk about Lindy's grief. She knew Abby would understand, first of all because it had been only THREE years since Abby's parents got divorced. And Abby's mom had proven herself to be no slouch in the snot-and-tear-producing category. Plus, just last summer, Abby and Bess had the (boo-hiss) Jonas refresher course on hysterically heartbroken moms, while Cristy had been in a state of perpetual car sickness driving through the Ozarks on "vacation" with her dad.

Bess listened to Lindy's sobs and almost leaked a tear of her own, imagining a long, lonely future without her old pal Abby to suffer through stuff with. But she couldn't, wouldn't, didn't call her.

She didn't call Cristy either, because Bess figured Cristy would think it was *good* news that Er-*ick* was gone, seeing as Bess had constantly complained about him. And it *was* good—just not *all* good.

Cristy's mom had been divorced since before Cristy could remember. And since Cristy had never heard her own mom crying over a broken heart, Bess figured Cristy couldn't really be expected to get it.

So, Bess didn't talk to anyone. From time to time she'd knock lightly on her mom's bedroom door and bring in cups of tea that Lindy wouldn't drink, and she lovingly arranged plates of apple slices and cheese that Lindy wouldn't eat, no matter how prettily Bess had folded the napkin. (Gilda taught her how when she'd worked as a set-up girl in a bistro.)

Sunday passed *very* slowly for everyone. We might as well just wait here at the end of this chapter, just to get the feel of how s-l-o-w-l-y time can pass.

Still waiting.

Waiting some more.

Sigh.

Chapter Twelve

awwww

So, by the time Monday came, neither Bess nor Abby could stand it anymore. They took one look at each other on the steps of the school that morning, and they smiled shyly and both said, "Sor-ry." (Which might make a good title, don't you think???)

Then Cristy came up and said, "Me too!" And the THREE of them threw their arms around one another and had a THREE-way hug. Other kids started yelling insults at them, but they just cheerfully flipped them off.

Maybe you're thinking, That's *all*??? No big dramatic emotional scene? And you're right. This probably *would* be a more meaningful story if the girls discussed their true feelings and regrets, their pains and confusions. Then we'd see that they'd grown intellectually and spiritually and had become better people with deeper, richer inner lives. Sadder but wiser, older but fatter, this-er but that-er. And the story could have a *moral*! Lots of narrators seem to go in for that sort of thing.

And we could stick in a part where the girls talk (subtly, without sounding message-y or preachy) about terribly important stuff like the value of friendship or something, and one of the girls (Bess?) could say that their THREE mothers were perfect examples of how hard it is to find love, and "that's why we friends need to stick together," or whatever.

Yeah, look! 1) Lindy's misery would be the cautionary tale (warning us not to jump through hoops to try to get some creep to like us). And 2) Abby's mom's romance with Steve would be there to prove that success is possible (at least so far). And 3) (THREE) Cristy's mom shows the independent, nonromance option because she's happy on her own. Isn't that tidy? Doesn't it sound planned out? Do I get credit for that even if it was totally by accident?

And this would be a good time for one of the girls to say something really, really touching. Something bittersweet and heartstring pulling, so *we* can maybe have a bit of a cry and feel all warm and fuzzy about the THREE friends and about ourselves. That's always popular. People totally love a happy cry.

But really all they said was "Sor-ry," and that's the truth.

It's the *truth,* but it's not the *end,* because something else happens in chapter THIRTEEN. Actually, *two* things happen.

(I suppose I could come up with a THIRD thing to stick in there, but this whole business with the THREES has really gotten on my nerves. Once you've started with that sort of thing, though, it's hard to stop no matter how majorly annoying it has become, and whether or not you can even remember why you thought it was such a good idea in the first place.)

Chapter THIRTEEN

the ending

The first (of the two things that happened) was this: Bess called Abby a couple of weeks (not THREE) after the hugging on the school steps and said, "Lindy met a new Er-*ick* in the ice cream section of the grocery store."

And Abby said, "Another one named *Eric*?"

"No, his name is . . . I can't remember," Bess said, shrugging (although Abby, obviously, couldn't see her). "And Lindy went blond today."

"Well, that's good, isn't it?" Abby asked. "Isn't blond better than roots?"

"That depends." Bess giggled. "Depends what this one is going to make her do. Play tuba at sunrise to worship some loo-loo who knows what? Paint the apartment mud brown and burn all the furniture?"

"At least he likes ice cream!" Abby said. But she wondered why it was that Lindy changed so much for men. So far, if Abby's own mom had changed, it was only that she smiled more and had started singing in the shower. (See? See? I got a useful message into this story after all! About how Abby's mom stayed true to herself and found happiness without dyeing her hair or chanting or whatever.)

Hey! How about *This Story* as the title? Since that's what I call it anyway. Then if I write another one later, it could be called *A Whole Nother Story*. Or I could call this *Story #1* and the next one *Story #2*! Wouldn't that be cute?

No, no! This one should be *Story #3*, because of all the THREENESS. And the next one I write could be *Story #2,* counting down like a rocket launch! Then I'd just have to write one more, and *blast off*!!! It would be a TRILOGY! A THREE-story collection sold in attractive gift boxes for the holidays!!! And I'd be rich! rich! rich! beyond my wildest dreams!!!$$$$$!

Seriously, we're getting pretty close to the end here, so a decision really, really *has* to be made now-ish, title-wise.

But more important than the title, and even more important than Lindy meeting an ice cream eater, is *the punch line!* The surprise ending that you're not even remotely prepared for!

Maybe that's not fair. Maybe I should scroll back and insert sneaky clues here and there, in the other chapters. But I'm not going to, and here's why: *No one* saw this ending coming, not Bess, not Abby, not even Cristy. No one had the least teeniest speck of a suspicion.

Oh, all right, I'll go back and drop one itty-bitty hint, and here's a hint about the hint: It's in chapter THREE. (Really.)

Here's a second (bonus) hint about the hint: It's about Cristy.

You can go back and check if you want, but hurry!

Time's up.

So: Remember how all this time Cristy had never felt the crush of a crushing crush, and she hadn't really understood all the fuss about the Bess-Fred-Emma thing?

Well, crush or no, she *had* been getting sort of used to Zack in her own way. Back when he was boyfriend-girlfriend with Bess, Cristy had loved going to his soccer games. And since they were in the same science class, Cristy and Zack sometimes worked on projects together. That's when they discovered that they were both huge Jim Carrey fans. And of all the Jim Carrey movies, they *both* liked *The Mask* best.

So one day, more than THREE (sorry, that slipped) weeks after Bess and Abby made up on the school steps, Cristy and Zack found themselves cracking up so hard together over a line from the new Jim Carrey movie that tears came to their eyes and they fell over.

"I can't wait to see it again!" Cristy wailed, her face sore from laughing.

"Me neither," Zack said. Then he added, "Wanna go together this weekend?"

And Cristy said, "Sure!"

And that was that.

It wasn't until hours later that Cristy thought, Uh-oh. Now I've gotta tell Abby and Bess. They'll kill me! They'll hate me forever! They'll I-don't-know-what!!!

But they didn't.

—Period, The End—

Epilogue

summation, apology,
and (another) confession

*H*aving just read this story, my sister, Bess (yes, you guessed it, I'm Gilda), says that 1) I got everything wrong and made her look way too mean. 2) She thinks the whole ABC and 123 thing is lame and she wants me to change her name to Lucretia. And 3) (THREE—oops!) She says they think Zack is a total dweeb and now just the mention of his (real) name makes all THREE girls flop around gagging and pretending to vomit. So there you go.

And that is totally the absolute *end* except for a couple of things I just want to tell you real quick. 1) Mr. Wordsmith is a fantastic teacher and I've learned tons and tons in his class! 2) I can't remember what the second thing was right now, but 3) (THREE) Apology: I'm sorry, but there were a few tiny things here that I *did* have to make up because (confession) I wasn't actually everywhere all the time. Please don't be mad.

Oh yeah, 2) was that Abby's bangs grew back kind of spiky and looked really cute . . . eventually.

(Note: Mr. Wordsmith came up with the title *Gossip Times THREE*. Isn't it great?)